UNDISCOVERED TREASURES

What Reviewers Say About MJ Williamz's Work

Exposed

"The love affair between Randi and Eleanor goes along in fits and starts. It is a wonderful story, and the sex is hot. Definitely read it as soon as you have a chance!"—Janice Best, Librarian (Albion District Library)

Shots Fired

"MJ Williamz, in her first romantic thriller, has done an impressive job of building the tension and suspense. Williamz has a firm grasp of keeping the reader guessing and quickly turning the pages to get to the bottom of the mystery. *Shots Fired* clearly shows the author's ability to spin an engaging tale and is sure to be just the beginning of great things to follow as the author matures."
—*Lambda Literary Review*

"Williamz tells her story in the voices of Kyla, Echo, and Detective Pat Silverton. She does a great job with the twists and turns of the story, along with the secondary plot. The police procedure is first rate, as are the scenes between Kyla and Echo, as they try to keep their relationship alive through the stress and mistrust."
—*Just About Write*

Forbidden Passions

"*Forbidden Passions* is 192 pages of bodice ripping antebellum erotica not so gently wrapped in the moistest, muskiest pantalets

of lesbian horn dog high jinks ever written. While the book is joyfully and unabashedly smut, the love story is well written and the characters are multi-dimensional. ...*Forbidden Passions* is the very model of modern major erotica, but hidden within the sweet swells and trembling clefts of that erotica is a beautiful May–September romance between two wonderful and memorable characters."
—*Rainbow Reader*

Sheltered Love

"The main pair in this story is astoundingly special, amazingly in sync nearly all the time, and perhaps the hottest twosome on a sexual front I have read to date. ...This book has an intensity plus an atypical yet delightful original set of characters that drew me in and made me care for most of them. Tantalizingly tempting!"
—*Rainbow Book Reviews*

Speakeasy

"*Speakeasy* is a bit of a blast from the past. It takes place in Chicago when Prohibition was in full flower and Al Capone was a name to be feared. The really fascinating twist is a small speakeasy operation run by a woman. She was more than incredible. This was such great fun and I most assuredly recommend it. Even the bloody battling that went on fit with the times and certainly spiced things up!"
—*Rainbow Book Reviews*

"In the Bell Tower" in *Women of the Dark Streets*

"New Orleans and a sexy female vampire helps an awkward visitor blossom and make sweet, sweet love all night long. Delicious!"
—*Rainbow Book Reviews*

Heartscapes

"The development of the relationship was well told and believable. Now the sex actually means something and MJ Williamz certainly knows how to write a good sex scene. Just when you think life has finally become great again for Jesse, Odette has a stroke and can't remember her at all. It is heartbreaking. Odette was a lovely character and I thought she was well developed. She was just the right person at the right time for Jesse. It was an engaging book, a beautiful love story."—*Inked Rainbow Reads*

By the Author

Shots Fired

Forbidden Passions

Initiation by Desire

Speakeasy

Escapades

Sheltered Love

Summer Passion

Heartscapes

Love on Liberty

Love Down Under

Complications

Lessons in Desire

Hookin' Up

Score

Exposed

Broken Vows

Model Behavior

Scene of the Crime

Thief of the Heart

Desires After Dark

Hearts in the Wind

Undiscovered Treasures

Undiscovered Treasures

by

MJ Williamz

2023

UNDISCOVERED TREASURES

ISBN 13: 978-1-63679-449-5

This Trade Paperback Original Is Published By
Bold Strokes Books, Inc.
P.O. Box 249
Valley Falls, NY 12185

First Edition: May 2023

CREDITS
Editor: Cindy Cresap
Production Design: Susan Ramundo
Cover Design By Tammy Seidick and Tina Michelle

Acknowledgments

As usual, a huge thank you to my wife, Laydin Michaels, for her never-ending support and encouragement in my writing and life.

Thank you so much to my beta readers—Sarah, Sue, and Sherri.

And a very special thank you to the talented Tina Michele whose design for my cover is what the final cover is based on.

Thanks, as always, to the crew at BSB for giving my stories a home.

Dedication

To all who follow their dreams

CHAPTER ONE

Wear linen, they told her. You'll be comfortable. Yeah, right. There was no way to be comfortable in the sauna that was Tampa at the end of May. It was over ninety degrees out and the humidity was off the charts. Cyl wanted to get back to her air-conditioned hotel room and peel her sticky clothes off. One thing was for sure, she wasn't in Fort Collins anymore.

She found the office in Ybor City. She had no idea what she was doing there. Something about Aunt Marjorie dying. But that's all she knew. She still didn't understand why whatever had to be said couldn't have been said over the phone. But the woman she spoke to had been insistent. So here she was.

"Cyl Waterford?" a pert admin assistant said.

"That's me."

"Thank you for coming. Can I get you anything? Coffee? Water?"

"I'd kill for a bottle of water," said Cyl.

"Wait right here. I'll be back in a sec."

She returned with the water and Cyl took a long drink. The coolness felt good on her insides and the air-conditioning had her outsides slowly evolving from a melted state.

"Can you tell me why I'm here?" Cyl said.

"I can't. But Martinique can. She'll see you now. Follow me."

The old building had Cyl assuming the inside would be dark and dismal, but quite the contrary. It was spacious and tastefully decorated in light blues and grays and yellows. Too femmey for her tastes, but it wasn't uncomfortable anyway.

A dark-haired beauty stood from behind a steel and glass desk.

"Cyl Waterford? Thank you so much for coming. I'm Martinique Thibideaux. We spoke on the phone?"

"Right." Cyl shook her outstretched hand. "I'm still not sure why I had to fly down here."

"I'm hoping I can answer all your questions now that you're here. Please. Sit down."

Martinique wore a form-fitting black dress. Cyl felt underdressed in her gray linen suit with her blue oxford underneath. She should have worn a tie. Oh, well.

"As we discussed on the phone, your aunt, Marjorie O'Connor, has passed away."

Cyl nodded slightly.

"I'm sorry to hear that, as I said, but I don't understand what that has to do with me."

"You weren't very close." It was a statement. Not a question.

"No. Apparently, there was some falling out between her and my parents."

"Yes. But she followed you from a distance. She was very proud of who you grew into."

"An architect?" Cyl laughed. "Not sure there's all that much to be proud of."

"You were your own person. Always. And that impressed her. At any rate, the reason you're here is she made you the executor of her will."

Cyl felt like she'd been punched in the gut. She didn't need this added responsibility. Especially from someone she didn't even know.

"So I have to have a meeting? Call friends and family? What does that mean?"

Martinique gave Cyl a soothing smile.

"No. It just means you'll be in charge of her will. You'll essentially carry out her final wishes."

"Still not sure why she picked me, but okay. Where do I find her will? When can we get started?"

"We can get started right now," said Martinique. "I drew up her will and I will now give it to you. Read it over. Take your time. Process everything. Ask any questions you have."

Cyl, proud of always being in control, fought shaking hands as she opened the envelope. The contents of the will were quite simple. Aunt Marjorie had left everything to Cyl. She looked up from the will.

"I don't understand," she said. "Why me?"

"Your aunt was quite fond of you, as I've said."

"I haven't heard from her in my entire life. How fond could she have been?"

"Very."

Cyl leaned back and took another sip of the cool water. Nothing was making sense. Some woman, an aunt who had had a disagreement with Cyl's parents way back when, thought enough of Cyl to leave her all her worldly possessions? Why would she do that?

"What's this about a lighthouse?" Cyl said.

"Marjorie owns the Old Murphy Lighthouse. And the attached cottage. Or she did, rather. You own them now."

"What the hell am I supposed to do with a lighthouse?"

"Whatever you'd like. Would you like to go see it?"

No, Cyl wanted to rail. No! She wanted to go back to Colorado where she belonged.

"I suppose I should," she said.

"Great. I'll have Donna drive you over there."

"Donna?"

"You met her when you first came in."

"Ah." Cyl nodded, still feeling like she'd wake from this bizarre dream any minute now.

Donna poked her head in.

"Ready when you are."

"I guess there's no time like the present," said Cyl. "Let's check this out."

Donna drove southwest out of Ybor City to Tampa proper. The antique-looking buildings gave way to modern neighborhoods. She continued until they arrived at a real, honest to goodness lighthouse on a rocky point.

The lighthouse sat on the narrow strip with the cottage nestled just behind it. Both the cottage and lighthouse were painted white, and each had a red roof. They were quite charming, if more than a little worn.

In the driveway off the cottage was a vintage car. It was huge, painted purple and black, and had fins. It was Cyl's dream car.

"There's her DeSoto," Donna said. "It was her pride and joy."

"I can see why," Cyl breathed reverently. "May I?"

"Sure. It's probably yours now anyway, am I right?"

Cyl fished the will out of her jacket pocket. The car was indeed hers. Hot damn.

"The keys are probably in the house," said Donna. "Let's check it out."

Cyl followed Donna up the crushed shell walkway to the red front door. Donna handed Cyl the keys.

"You should do the honors."

Cyl unlocked the door and let herself into the cute, sparsely decorated cottage. The entry hall had wood floors that desperately needed to be redone. The spacious living room had one beige leather couch, a wide-screen television, and shelves and shelves of books.

Though she'd never been much of a reader herself, Cyl was drawn to the volumes lining the walls. There were murder mysteries, historical books on pirates and the area, and lots of general books about the sea, some fiction, some not.

When Cyl took a moment to step back from the books, she became faintly aware of a sour smell. She realized it was her.

"Does this place have AC?" she said.

"Sure. I think the thermostat's in the dining room."

Cyl found it and cranked the cool air. She breathed a sigh of relief.

"Much better," she said. She saw the car keys on the dining room table. "Shall we see if she runs?"

"Of course she does. Marjorie took excellent care of old Mabel."

"Mabel?" Cyl was sure her dead aunt would be okay with her renaming the beauty.

"Would you like to follow me back to the office? I know Martinique cleared her calendar in case you had questions or anything."

"Sure. I'll meet you back there." Cyl really wished she could swing by her hotel and take a quick shower. Tampa was killing her and she'd only been there a few hours. Oh, well. She'd take one later.

Martinique was waiting when they returned.

"Well? What did you think?" she said.

"It's cute. What I saw. It definitely needs some work. Which I'm up for."

"What will you do with it, Cyl?"

"I plan to fix it up and sell it."

"Sell it?" Martinique didn't try to hide her surprise.

"I'm not cut out for this kind of heat and humidity. I just can't see me living here."

"Fair enough. Do you have any questions or anything you need from me?"

"If I may," said Cyl. "How did she die? She couldn't have been that old."

"She was in her seventies. And she died of a brain aneurysm. She went very quickly."

Cyl was happy to hear that. Even if she didn't know the crazy aunt who'd left everything to her, she didn't want to think of her suffering.

"And she didn't have a husband? No one she was close to?"

Martinique shook her head.

"Nope. Oh, she was well loved. Don't fool yourself into believing she was a lonely old spinster." Martinique laughed. "She was a character. Everybody knew and loved Marjorie. But she kept everyone at an arm's distance as she grew older."

"I wonder why?"

"There are rumors. She'd fallen in love when she was in her forties. It came to an end about ten years ago. Why? No one seems to know. From that point on, Marjorie was more guarded. But, listen to me, I'm gossiping. I apologize."

"No need to apologize. It's all good. I appreciate your candor."

"Are you hungry? I know a great Cuban restaurant within walking distance."

"That sounds amazing. But I'd really like to take a shower before I go out in public."

"Nonsense. You look great. Let's go."

It was six thirty and still ungodly hot and muggy. So very muggy. Cyl wanted to hurry Martinique along to get to the air-conditioned restaurant, but she wouldn't be hurried. She was regaling Cyl with stories of the neighborhood and its history. Apparently, the whole block had once been a cigar factory. Cyl really enjoyed listening to Martinique even as she wilted yet again.

Her stomach growled loudly as they entered the cool, dark restaurant. It smelled divine. Cyl couldn't wait to eat, but as they waited to be seated, she took in the décor and realized they were supposed to be in a pirate ship. What was it with these people and pirates?

"The pirate ship atmosphere is a nice touch," she said. "I noticed my aunt had a lot of books about pirates as well. Is that a thing around here?"

Martinique laughed.

"Have you never heard of Jose Gaspar?"

"Can't say that I have."

"He's a big name around these parts. Famous pirate. We celebrate him every January with a parade and festival."

"No kidding?"

"Scout's honor."

They were seated and Cyl did her best to decipher the menu. It all sounded amazing. She'd never had Cuban food before. If it tasted as good as the smells wafting through the restaurant, she was going to be in for a treat.

"So how long do you think you'll stay in Tampa?" said Martinique.

"However long it takes. Probably a few months. We'll see."

"I'm sorry you won't be living in the lighthouse. It would be nice to keep it in the family."

"Sorry to disappoint, but as I said, I don't think Tampa is for me."

"I think you should taste the nightlife. You might be surprised."

"I suppose I might. But I doubt it cools off much here at night, and it's the heat that's killing me."

"Not the humidity?"

"Okay," Cyl laughed. "The humidity definitely doesn't help."

After dinner, they walked back to the office where Cyl got in Mabel.

"Thanks for a nice evening. I enjoyed myself," she said.

"You're quite welcome. It was my pleasure. You sure I can't talk you into a nightcap?"

"I think I'll head back to the hotel and pack up to move my stuff to the cottage. Thanks though."

"Well, if you ever need anything, you have my number."

"I do indeed. I do have one question for another night. Where would one find a women's club around here?"

"Oh, my. The apple didn't fall far from the family tree."

"What do you mean?" said Cyl.

"Your aunt may have lived alone much of her life, but she never wanted for the attention of a beautiful woman."

"Is that right?"

"Mm-hm. Oh. And you want Seventh Avenue. That's where you'll find whatever it is you're looking for."

"Thanks for the tip. Good night."

Martinique smiled and closed Cyl's door. Cyl wondered how often Martinique frequented Seventh Avenue. Maybe she'd run into the attractive Martinique again sometime.

CHAPTER TWO

It took Cyl a few minutes to recognize where she was the following morning. She woke with the sun and the shadows in the room were unfamiliar and more than a little disorienting. Then it all came back to her. She was sleeping in her aunt's cottage. Correction. Her cottage. She owned it. And she couldn't wait to flip it.

She found the coffee pot and took her coffee to the lighthouse. She climbed the spiral staircase to the gallery at the top. The view was impressive. She sat in an Adirondack chair and gazed out at the Gulf of Mexico. It was serene at that moment, and she wondered why the lighthouse had ever been needed in that spot.

Then she remembered where she was. Florida. Home of heat, humidity, and hurricanes. Surely the gulf could get rough when the winds blew strong. She wondered what the lighthouse had been like in its heyday. She found herself wondering when it was built. Then she asked herself why she cared. She was going to fix it, sell it, and get out of Dodge.

Cyl noticed the worn wood as she climbed down the stairs en route to another cup of coffee. She'd have to replace them. And the walls. They looked like they could cave in at any moment. She had her work cut out for her. Fortunately, she was a very successful architect and her aunt had also left her a tidy sum. Fixing up the place could be fun. And it wouldn't devastate her financially.

She browsed the library while sipping her coffee. She wouldn't have time to read while she was there but was curious about the lighthouse and its history. Even though she told herself she didn't care, her curiosity won, and she found a book on Florida lighthouses.

Making herself comfortable on the couch, she read about the original Florida lighthouse in St. Augustine. Apparently, it had been built in 1824. So this one was only a couple of hundred years old. Hm. Somehow she was thinking it would have been built in the sixteen hundreds when the pirates Martinique had told her about had been in the area. Oh, well.

Cyl found the chapter on Old Murphy Lighthouse and found it had been there since 1830. She was somewhat fascinated and found that she wanted to know more about the area, its history and such. Then she reminded herself, yet again, that she had work to do and couldn't spend the whole day lollygagging over books and coffee.

After her shower, she decided her first order of business would be to tackle the master bedroom. She hadn't minded sleeping in the guest room the night before, but she felt she'd be happier in the more spacious master.

As she stripped the bed, she realized she hadn't asked Martinique if Aunt Marjorie had died at home. That kind of creeped her out a little. She got over it quickly and stripped the bedding, started laundry, and went back to see if she needed to make any other changes in there to make her stay more comfortable.

Cyl checked out the photos on the dresser. She recognized pictures of her mother as a young girl. And her grandmother. That must have been Marjorie with them. The pictures brought up unpleasant feelings so she put them in a drawer to be dealt with later.

How could her mother have disowned her own sister? Her only sibling? The same way she'd disowned her only daughter. Homosexuality was too much scandal for her to bear. What a fucking bitch.

She moved to the large oak desk that she thought she'd use as a drafting table. It, too, had pictures on it, but they were more recent. These photos showed Marjorie smiling and laughing and always surrounded by women or drag queens. Cyl had to laugh. She wished she could have met her aunt while she was still alive. She was sure they would have hit it off.

She finished clearing off the desk and cleaning out its drawers. She wondered if there was anyone in particular who might be interested in any of the things Cyl had come across. She would take care of the old bank statements and tax forms, but there were mementos, knick-knacky things that someone might want. She made a mental note to ask around.

It was after ten and she hadn't eaten. She decided it was time to take Mabel for a spin around town and find a diner for breakfast. She drove around until she got herself good and lost. She wanted to go back to the neighborhood where Martinique's office was. If only she could remember what it was called. She was sure Martinique had said the name.

Ybor City. It came to her. She googled breakfast in Ybor City, found a restaurant, and let Siri guide her. As she approached the front door, she noticed several employees staring at her from just outside.

"Is something wrong?" Cyl tried to sound friendly rather than annoyed.

"That's Marjorie's car," and older buxom woman said.

"I'm her niece. She left me the car."

"You're Marjorie's niece? Come in, come in. Breakfast is on the house this morning."

The older woman pulled Cyl into a bear hug, which left Cyl feeling confused, smothered, and claustrophobic.

"It's a pleasure to meet you. I'm Dolores. I'm the hostess and we loved your aunt here. Absolutely loved her."

"Thank you. That's nice to hear."

Cyl followed the group inside the diner where Dolores showed her to a table overlooking a large fountain. It was nice. Everything was nice, but Cyl was starved and all she could think about was eating.

She finished her breakfast and was sipping her last cup of coffee when an attractive brunette leaned on her booth.

"I understand you're Marjorie's niece," she said. She was tall, full-figured, and had deep brown eyes. Maybe being related to Marjorie would have its perks beyond a free breakfast.

"I am," said Cyl.

"I'm Luna. Luna Marchetti. I was a close friend of your aunt's. Let me just say how sorry I am for your loss."

"And I'm sorry for yours. My name's Cyl, by the way."

"Pleasure to meet you. May I buy your breakfast?"

"Thank you," said Cyl. "But it's already taken care of."

Luna smiled, showing perfect white teeth. She was a looker. No doubt about that.

"Of course. I doubt Dolores would take your money."

"No."

"When did you get in town?"

"Yesterday. I met with a Martinique Thibideaux. I guess she's handling my aunt's affairs? Or was. And now I am."

"Martinique is a sweetheart. I'm glad Marjorie used her. Not surprising though. Marjorie knew good people when she saw them. You must have been very special to her."

"I'm not sure, really," Cyl said.

"Don't be modest. Anyway. I'll leave you to your coffee. I'd like to get together with you and talk about things sometime."

"Things?"

Luna shrugged.

"The lighthouse, cottage, Mabel, life. Just visit with you."

"That would be great." And Cyl meant it. She definitely wanted to spend more time with Luna. Preferably not talking, but it had to start somewhere, she supposed. She took out her phone. "What's your number?"

She gave Luna her number as well and said good-bye. She watched Luna leave the restaurant and brought herself back from fantasyland to the work she had in front of her.

First order of business would be renting a truck. She'd need one to haul lumber and other supplies. Besides, she'd be more comfortable driving a truck around than Mabel. She would be crushed if anything happened to her. And apparently, so would half of Ybor City.

She left enough money on the table to have covered her meal and went to the front and thanked Dolores for her hospitality. She also inquired about a truck rental in the area. Dolores gave her the name of one and Cyl left, ready to get on with her life.

Cyl was tired when she got back to the cottage with the truck. Her Uber driver had almost killed her getting to the rental place, and then she had to fight Tampa traffic to get home. Her nerves were shot and it was only one o'clock. She wanted a drink. A stiff drink. But it was too early. Still, she thought she'd like to go exploring that night. She called Martinique.

"Hello?"

"Martinique? It's Cyl Waterford. We met yesterday?"

"Of course. How are you? Is everything okay?"

"Yeah. Everything is great. I just wondered if you'd mind showing this tourist the hot spots tonight?"

"On a Wednesday night?" Martinique laughed. "I could do that. But I can't stay out late."

"Understood. Is there a place we can meet? And what time would work for you?"

"I can close up a little early," said Martinique. "Let's meet at the Old Irish Pub on Eighth at four."

"I'll be there. Thanks, Martinique."

"Thank you for thinking of me. I'll make sure you have a good time."

"Appreciate that." But Martinique had already disconnected. Cyl wondered just how good of a time Martinique would show her. She could use a little extracurricular activity to burn some energy.

Cyl went to her room to unpack. She looked at the pile of Marjorie's clothes on the bed and told herself to ask Martinique what to do with them. In the meantime, she needed to find a place to store them.

She searched the house until she found some large garbage bags in the laundry room. She carefully folded the clothes and filled four bags. Then she hung her nice clothes and filled the top two drawers of the dresser with shorts, underwear, and T-shirts.

Next, Cyl got her MacBook situated on her desk and began jotting down notes of things she already knew needed to be dealt with. The wood panels inside the lighthouse and the staircase were on the top of her list.

Cyl hiked back up to the top of the lighthouse again, noting which steps would need to be replaced and which panels were in the worst shape. She got to the sun-drenched gallery and braced herself for the heat.

But instead of hot, it was surprisingly cool. Like someone had turned the air conditioner on. But there was no AC on that floor. Odd. She checked out all the windows, but they were sealed. There was no breeze coming from anywhere. By the time she'd checked everything, the room was hot again.

Cyl wondered what the hell was going on but didn't ponder it long. She had a shower to take and an attractive woman to meet for drinks. She put the incident out of her mind and headed to the shower.

A pub. What did one wear to a pub? Shorts would be okay surely. She put on khaki cargo shorts and sat on the bed trying to figure out what shirt to put on. If they went dancing later, she'd need to look nice. But Martinique had said she couldn't stay late. So were they only going to have a few drinks at the pub?

Why was she perseverating so? Because she wanted to get laid. That's what she was hoping for. And that wouldn't happen if she didn't look her best or if she underdressed and embarrassed Martinique.

She decided on a short-sleeved baby blue oxford shirt that she knew accentuated her eyes. She sprayed some Patrick cologne and was ready. She locked the door as her Uber arrived and she relaxed in the back seat. She was in for a good time that night. She could feel it in her bones.

CHAPTER THREE

Y ou didn't want to sit outside?" Martinique said when she joined Cyl at the pub.

"God no. I mean, the palm trees are nice and everything, but no thanks."

Martinique laughed.

"I'm just giving you a hard time. It's going to take a while for you to acclimate to Tampa."

"I don't plan on being here that long."

"That's too bad," said Martinique. "I think you'd fit in quite well here."

"I'll take my snow in the winter over the humidity down here."

"Suit yourself. What are you drinking?"

"A Guinness. It seems fitting. This place is nice. And empty. I suppose I'm not going to find much going on around here on a weeknight."

"You'd be surprised. This little section of the world is jumpin' every night. There's always a DJ somewhere, and where there's a DJ there's dancing."

"Do you dance?" Cyl said.

"Of course. But not on a Wednesday night. I'll still show you where to find the action and leave you to your own devices."

"I think I'd have more fun if you were with me."

"Then ask me on a date."

"Isn't this a date?" said Cyl.

"I don't know. You tell me."

"I'd like it to be." Cyl hoped she didn't sound desperate.

"So would I."

"With that settled, may I buy you a drink?"

They moved from the bar to a table where they sat quietly sipping their drinks.

"There was something we didn't cover yesterday," said Martinique.

"What's that?"

"Marjorie's ashes."

Cyl fought through the regret that overwhelmed her. She didn't want to deal with her dead aunt's ashes. But she'd been so gracious to leave Cyl everything that she figured it was the least she could do.

"What about them?" she said.

"She'd like them scattered over the gulf. I think that's something you'll have to arrange."

"I suppose it is. Well, if that's what she wanted, I'll take care of it. Where are her ashes now?"

"At the office. I'll get them to you."

"Thank you.

"Okay. No more shop talk. I promise. Though I am curious how you like the cottage?" said Martinique.

"It's nice. It's worn for sure, and the lighthouse? I'm surprised it's still standing. But I'll get it in shipshape. No pun intended."

"Ha. Right."

Cyl had relaxed significantly. Martinique was so easy to be with. She had a calming presence that Cyl welcomed. Though she couldn't help but wonder what Martinique would be like in bed. Would she be a pillow princess? Or was she a tiger between the sheets?

"Penny for your thoughts," Martinique said.

"I'm afraid they're not worth that. Tell me about yourself. Are you a native Tampan? Is that what they're called?"

Martinique laughed. It was a magical sound and Cyl wanted to hear it again.

"That is indeed what we call ourselves. And I was born and raised in this great city."

"Have you traveled at all?"

"I've been all over the world. The only places I would live besides Tampa are Buenos Aires or New Orleans. But I'm happy here. Especially in Ybor City."

"Okay. I've got to ask. Since this is technically part of Tampa, why is it called Ybor City?" said Cyl.

"It was named after a Cuban cigar factory owner from the late eighteen hundreds. And the name stuck."

"Got it. Weird, but okay. So have your travels taken you to Colorado?"

"Indeed they have. I spent a summer in Estes Park. It was magical."

"Not much to do there."

"It was heaven. We hiked, fished, went on weekend trips to Denver. I was ten and it was one of my favorite summers ever," Martinique said.

"I love hiking and fishing. There's plenty of that to do there for sure."

"Oh yes. It was there I discovered my love of the great outdoors."

"But you can't really enjoy the outdoors here," said Cyl. "It's too hot and too humid."

"Depends on if you're tough or not." Martinique laughed.

"I like to think I'm pretty tough." Cyl smiled at her.

"Do ya now?"

"Mm-hm."

"Well, maybe I'll arrange for us to do an outdoor activity sometime before you hightail it out of here."

"We'll see," said Cyl. "We'll just see about that."

Martinique checked her watch.

"Do you need to get going?" Cyl's heart dropped.

"No. But this should be our last drink here. We need to find you some nightlife."

"But I'm really enjoying visiting with you. I don't mind staying here all night."

"Are you sure?"

"Positive."

"Okay. But I feel like I'm holding you hostage."

"You can hold me hostage any time," Cyl said.

Martinique arched an eyebrow.

"Is that right?"

"Yes, ma'am."

"I don't know about the hostage part, but why don't you buy me dinner and we can go to my place and see who's holding whom?"

"Do you mean that?" said Cyl.

"I do. Now, settle our tab and let's get some food."

"I suppose we'll walk to the restaurant?"

"Of course. It's a nice evening out," Martinique said.

"You call this nice? Are you a masochist?"

"That's for me to know and you to find out." Martinique laced her hand through Cyl's elbow. That touch had Cyl's head spinning. Blood rushed in her ears. She was going to have a lot of fun later. She was sure of that. She struggled to find something to say. Something that wouldn't make her sound like a blubbering fool. But her brain was short-circuiting.

"Are there any good steakhouses around here? Or do you even eat red meat?"

"I eat pink meat."

"Damn. Can we blow off dinner?"

"Negative. And yes. I love a good steak. I know just the place. Come on."

Dinner was superb, but it had done nothing to quell Cyl's desire. If anything, the hour and a half she'd spent at the restaurant had only served to whet her sexual appetite further. Martinique was beautiful and funny. But she was also intelligent. And that was the biggest turn-on for Cyl.

"My place isn't far from here if you can handle a little more walking," Martinique said.

"Lead the way."

Cyl walked with Martinique to a cute blue Craftsman a few blocks away from the hustle and bustle. It was adorable.

"This is yours?"

"Yes, ma'am. Mine all mine. It's not much, but I love it. Come on in. Would you like a nightcap?"

"I think I've had enough to drink," said Cyl.

"Then let me show you the bedroom."

Cyl liked that there was no pretense of showing off the house or any nonsense. They were both there for one reason and one reason only.

The bedroom was spacious and done in pale yellow. It was very feminine and was definitely Martinique's.

"This is nice." Cyl sat on the king-size bed and looked up at Martinique. She patted the bed next to her and Martinique sat. She was so close Cyl could feel the heat radiating off her.

Cyl leaned over and lightly brushed her lips against Martinique's.

"I've been wanting to do that all night," Cyl said.

"Only tonight? I wanted it the minute you walked into my office yesterday."

"Jet lag." Cyl laughed.

"Apology accepted. Now, please kiss me again. Like you mean it."

Cyl kissed Martinique again and Martinique opened her mouth and darted her tongue into Cyl's mouth. Cyl almost lost control. She wanted to rip Martinique's dress off her and have her every which way she could.

The next thing Cyl was conscious of, Martinique was on her back and Cyl was on top of her. Martinique wrapped her legs around Cyl's hips and Cyl thought she'd climax from the sheer wantonness of Martinique.

"Touch me, baby," Martinique whispered hoarsely.

"Now?"

"Yes."

Cyl slid her hand up Martinique's soft yet toned inner thigh and under her dress. Martinique had nothing on under and Cyl shuddered when her fingers met hot, wet flesh. Martinique was drenched and Cyl continued to caution herself to go slowly, even though Martinique seemed to have other ideas.

Martinique hiked her dress up over her hips making it easier for Cyl to tease her. She circled her clit over and over before plunging deep inside. Martinique was tight, so tight and Cyl squeezed her own legs together and reveled at the pressure on her own clit.

She moved lower on the bed so she could taste heaven. She ran her tongue over the length of Martinique who tasted divine. She buried her tongue as deep as she could, lapping all the juices she found. Her face was coated with Martinique's essence and still she couldn't get enough.

Martinique's clit stood at attention, poking out from the safety of its hood. Cyl took it in her mouth and ran her tongue over and under and around. Martinique gyrated on the bed. She placed her hand on the back of Cyl's head and pressed her further into her. Cyl could barely breathe but didn't care. All that mattered was the deliciousness in her mouth.

She sucked hard on Martinique's morsel until Martinique was bucking on the bed, raising her hips against Cyl's mouth. Cyl held on until Martinique screamed then collapsed back on the bed.

Cyl licked the remnants of her orgasm before rolling off to catch her breath.

"Why'd you stop?" said Martinique.

"You want more? I can go for more."

Cyl moved back between Martinique's legs. She licked deep within her again, stroking the soft silky spots she found there. She sucked her lips and cleaned them only to have more cream develop there.

She could have stayed here forever and somehow had the feeling that she was there for the duration of the night anyway. This didn't bother her. Martinique was tasty and fun. A wicked combination.

Cyl brought Martinique to another orgasm and was settling in for number three when Martinique spoke.

"That's enough for now," she said. "I just needed you to take the edge off."

"Fair enough. Now, can we get undressed?"

"No. I like sex with clothes on."

"But I'd love to see your whole body."

"Not gonna happen, lovergirl."

Cyl climbed up next to Martinique and played with her breasts through her dress. Martinique responded by unzipping Cyl's shorts.

"Can I get naked?" said Cyl.

"Nope. I'm gonna finger fuck you to oblivion."

Never one to stop a lady from enjoying herself, Cyl lay back and let Martinique have her way with her. Martinique's fingers were strong and demanding.

"You're so wet," said Martinique.

"Imagine that."

Martinique laughed. A deep, throaty sound that had Cyl teetering on the edge of reality,

She finally withdrew her fingers from inside Cyl and moved to her rigid clit.

"Damn. Your clit is huge."

"Again. Imagine that."

She stroked it expertly, pressing just under the sensitive tip and applying more and more pressure as she played. Cyl held her breath, knowing she was going to come any second. She closed her eyes tight as she clenched up, watched the light show burst before her eyelids, then sank back onto the bed, satiated, but still wanting more.

She wanted to see Martinique's body. She knew it was hot and wanted to see her flesh. Knowing she couldn't only made her want it more.

"Okay, Cyl," said Martinique as she sucked her fingers clean.

"Yes?"

"I work tomorrow so you'd better get going. Thanks for tonight. I really enjoyed myself."

"Can we do it again?"

"I make no promises. I'm not looking for a relationship right now. Especially not with someone from Colorado." She laughed.

"Fair enough. But there's chemistry between us. You've got to admit that. Just keep me in mind if you want a quickie or more. I'll be around for a few months."

"I have your number, Cyl. And you have mine. Good night."

"Walk me to the door?" said Cyl.

"Mm. I'm comfortable here. I'm sure you can find your way out."

"Good night, Martinique."

Cyl relived her evening on the way back to her house. It had been fun. Strange, but fun.

CHAPTER FOUR

Cyl was replacing the steps in the lighthouse when her phone buzzed in her pocket. Wondering who would be calling her, she looked at the phone and saw Luna. She answered it.

"Hello?"

"Cyl? It's Luna. I've been ringing your doorbell and you're not answering. I just wanted to make sure you were okay."

"Sorry. I'm working in the lighthouse. Give me a few and I'll let you in."

She opened the front door and saw Luna in a pair of short shorts and a tight T-shirt. Damn. Women here sure did something to her. They made it hard to think with her hormones raging.

"Come on in," said Cyl. "You want some coffee or something?"

"A cup of coffee would be nice."

"Let me start a pot. Have a seat at the dining room table and I'll be right with you."

Cyl walked back to the dining room and Luna looked like she was about to cry.

"Luna? Are you okay?"

"I am. I'm sorry. It's just sitting here like this, I expect Marjorie to come out of the kitchen with coffee so we can settle in for a long talk about anything and nothing."

"I see." Cyl nodded. "Well, I doubt I'm the conversationalist my aunt was, but I'll try."

Luna smiled.

"I'm sure you can hold your own."

"I hate to make a sore spot hurt more, but my aunt had a lot of knick-knacks and the like and I was wondering if you or someone you know might be interested in them?"

"Oh, how thoughtful. I'd love to look through them. Not now, of course."

"Why not now?"

"I don't want to take up too much of your time," said Luna.

"No worries. I'm not on a schedule."

"Okay. Then I'll take a look."

"Lots of photos, too," said Cyl. "Anything you want is yours."

"I appreciate that."

"She also had a ton of clothes. Do you know where she'd want them donated?"

"You didn't just throw them away?" Luna sounded surprised.

"I figured someone might need them. And my aunt sounds like the type who would have donated rather than tossed."

"That she was. How well did you know Marjorie?"

"To be honest, I didn't. My parents cut her out of their lives long before I was born. Every so often I'd hear something about my mother's sister, but not very often."

"That's a shame. She followed you from a very young age. Marjorie was quite intuitive. She sensed greatness in you."

Cyl laughed uncomfortably.

"I guess I disappointed then."

"Not at all. Your aunt was very proud of you, Cyl."

"Thank you. That's nice to hear."

"I'm sorry. I don't think I have it in me to go through Marjorie's things today. Would you be terribly upset if I asked to come back another day?"

"Not at all. I'm sure this is hard for you."

"It really is. Don't get me wrong, Cyl. You seem like a wonderful person. And you radiate great energy. But you're not Marjorie and it's going to take me a while to get used to Marjorie's death."

"Understood. May I ask you a favor?"

"Sure."

"I need to spread my aunt's ashes over the gulf," said Cyl. "Would you go with me?"

"I'd be honored."

Cyl got an interesting vibe from Luna. She seemed a little off, but Cyl couldn't quite pinpoint how and where. But she struck Cyl as odd. Nice enough. Easy on the eyes. But odd.

"I should go," said Luna. "Thanks for spending these few minutes with me."

"No worries. Any friend of my aunt's is a friend of mine. You're always welcome here."

"Thank you."

"Would you mind telling me who to donate her clothes to before you go?"

"I'll take them," said Luna. "There's a battered women's shelter Marjorie volunteered at. She'd love them to have her clothes, I'm sure. I'll take them."

"Thank you," said Cyl. "That would be great."

With Luna out of the house, Cyl went back to work on the staircase. As she worked, she let her mind wander back to Luna. She was very curious what her relationship was with her aunt. Were they lovers? Luna was around Cyl's age, so mid to late thirties. That would have been awfully young to be involved with her aunt. Or would it?

The more time she spent in Tampa, the more curious she became about her aunt. Who was she? Why had her parents disowned her? Was it because she was a lesbian? More than likely. She imagined her father had been the driving force behind that. Her mother, bitch though she was, would never turn against her own sister on her own. Or would she?

Whose idea had it been to cut Cyl out of the family? Sure, they stood as a united front, but Cyl was certain her retired military father had been the catalyst behind it. She didn't miss him or her mother, but her younger brother crossed her mind sometimes. She wondered how he was and if he ever thought about her.

Damn. She didn't need to be getting maudlin when she had work to do. She turned her attention back to the staircase and got it finished early evening. She wanted a beer but didn't want to be alone. She took a shower and headed back to the pub she'd visited with Martinique.

"Guinness?" the bartender said.

"Please."

She sat at the bar lost in her own head working out plans to get the cottage and lighthouse ready for the market when she felt a light touch on her shoulder. She turned to see Luna standing there.

"Luna. What a pleasant surprise."

"Hi, Cyl. A group of your aunt's friends are sitting over in the corner if you'd like to join us."

"Thanks, but I'd hate to intrude."

"No intrusion at all. We'd love to have you join us. We're still mourning her loss, so it may be slightly somber. But we'd love you to come sit with us."

Sitting with a bunch of morose strangers did not sound like a good time. But Cyl could find no excuse not to.

"Sure. I'll join you guys."

There were five other women at the table. All varying ages, but they all brightened when Cyl walked up.

"You're Marjorie's niece?" one older woman said. "Welcome. Please sit down."

Cyl took a seat at the cramped table. The older woman introduced herself as Madeline. Cyl shook her outstretched hand.

"Nice to meet you," Cyl said.

"Madeline was one of Marjorie's lovers," said Luna.

"Oh." Cyl wasn't sure how to respond to this statement. "I'm so sorry for your loss."

"Thank you," said Madeline. "It wasn't like I was the only one though. Your aunt's appetite for sex was legendary."

Cyl felt herself blush at the comment that hit too close to home. The rest of the women laughed though, so Cyl relaxed.

"Madeline meant the world to your aunt," said another older woman. "They were fantastic together. Don't let her modesty fool you. I'm Nadine, by the way."

"So you were an item?" Cyl was confused. "Or not?"

"Your aunt refused to be tied down after the love of her life left her. No one was an item with Marjorie after she turned fifty-three."

"I see. I'm sorry she got hurt. That breaks my heart."

"She was a very resilient woman," said Nadine. "But when Louise left her for a younger woman, the walls around her heart went up. And never came back down."

"How long were she and Louise together?"

"Thirty years. They met when they were in college," Luna said. "Louise insisted that they'd gotten together too young and that she had seeds to sow that she hadn't been able to. So she left."

"Is she still in the area?"

Nadine said, "No. She and her chippy moved to Asheville. Good riddance if you ask me."

"I'm sure," said Cyl.

She wanted to hunt down Louise and exact some form of revenge on the part of her aunt. But she knew she was just caught up in the moment. Or was she? The more she learned about her aunt, the more she wanted to know.

"I appreciate you guys sharing stories with me," she said. "As I'm sure you know, I didn't know her at all."

"That's unfortunate," said Madeline. "She adored you. And was so proud of you. She almost reached out to you when your parents disowned you. Obviously, she could relate."

"I wonder why she didn't?"

"She didn't want to interfere with your life. You were your own person and she wanted to watch you grow and become who you needed to be without any interference."

"Still. It would have been nice to have known my benefactor."

"I'm sure," said Luna.

"I'll buy the next round," said Cyl. "Who needs a refill?"

Three of the women raised their empties and Cyl called the bartender over. Drinks refreshed, the conversation at the table died down.

"I should leave you now," said Cyl. "I've taken enough of your time."

"No," said Madeline. "Please stay. It's like having a piece of Marjorie with us."

"Okay. But only until I finish this beer. Then I'm off to find some dinner."

"May I join you? If you don't mind?" A lovely blonde at the end of the table finally spoke. Cyl had no idea who she was or why she'd want dinner with her, but she felt it would be rude to say no.

"I don't mind at all. And you are?"

"I'm Tawny. I'd love to spend some one-on-one time with you. As sort of a grasping last connection with Marjorie."

"Sure. I'll even buy."

Tawny blushed.

"No need. It'll be my treat. It's the least I can do after inviting myself along."

Cyl and Tawny bid adieu to the rest of the women and Cyl braced herself to step outside. It did no good. The muggy oven she stepped into hit her with a force no matter how she tried to prepare herself for it.

Tawny was wearing a pair of short-shorts and a spaghetti strap top that did little to support her luscious breasts. Shit. This woman was in mourning and Cyl was checking her out. She really was a dog.

"Is there someplace casual we can go?" said Cyl. "I'm not really dressed for fancy."

"Do you like Cuban sandwiches?"

"I've never had one."

"Great. You're in for a treat."

They finished their sandwiches and the silence was deafening. Cyl knew she had to get going, but Tawny seemed like she might break into tears any moment.

"I guess I should get going," she finally said.

"May I ask another favor?"

"Sure."

"May I come over and see the lighthouse and cottage some day? I miss hanging out there."

"Sure. When would you like to come over?"

"What are you doing tonight?"

"You want to come over now?"

"I'm sorry. That was awfully bold of me."

"No. That's fine. I have no plans tonight. Why don't we pick up a bottle of wine and head over there. You're okay to drive, aren't you?"

"I am. Let's go."

They arrived back at the cottage and Tawny's voice cracked as she stood in the entry hall.

"I'm sorry. It's just I expect Marjorie to come around the corner."

"It's okay." Cyl hugged Tawny. "It's okay. If you need to cry, you go right ahead."

Tawny took a deep breath and pulled back after a few moments.

"I'll be fine. Thank you though. You're so much like Marjorie it's like being in her presence. It really is."

"I think I'll take that as a compliment."

"That's exactly how it was intended."

"Come on in. I'll pour the wine." Cyl filled their glasses. "I really wish I had known my aunt. Everyone's stories about her are so filled with love and real caring."

"We all loved her. Everyone did. And she loved everyone. She was a very special person indeed."

Chapter Five

I have some of Aunt Marjorie's things boxed up if you'd like to look through them. Luna said she would, but I thought I'd offer some to you, as well."

"Thank you. That's very sweet," said Tawny. "I would love to take a look."

"How did you know my aunt?" Cyl put a box on the table for Tawny to look through.

"I work in a bookstore. She used to come in all the time. She kind of took me under her wing."

"That's sweet of her."

"It really was. She had such a big heart. Soon we were having coffee together and then she'd invite me over for game nights. She was like a surrogate mother to me."

"That's really cool," said Cyl. "I'm glad you had each other."

"You're just like what I imagined she would have been as a younger woman."

"Is that right?"

Tawny nodded.

"I can't speak for the others, of course, but I'd bet they feel the same."

"It's an honor that you feel that way. I'm afraid I'm not as selfless as she seemed to be. But I try."

"You're very kind to all of us. You didn't have to join us at the pub, but you did. And you listened to the stories and participated in the conversation. Perhaps you're more selfless than you realize."

Cyl shrugged.

"Maybe." But she knew she wasn't. She always thought about herself first. She was always looking out for number one. She doubted if she died that they'd find three people to mourn her. Maybe it wasn't too late to change? She'd have to see.

Tawny was holding a ceramic dolphin in her hands.

"I gave this to her. She loved dolphins. I gave it to her years ago. May I keep it?"

"Sure," said Cyl. "Take whatever you'd like."

"So much of this reminds me of her. I'm sorry they're not still up and spread around the house."

"They're not really my style."

"I get that." Tawny's eyes lit up. "We should play a game."

"A game?" Cyl wasn't into board games or anything like that. She wondered how far she'd go to amuse Tawny. "I'm not really into games."

"Do you play cards?"

"Sure."

"Let's play poker."

"For money?" Cyl was surprised at the suggestion.

"Let's make it interesting."

"I'm listening."

"Strip poker."

"Tawny. If we get naked…I have to be honest here. I'm only human. And you're very attractive. I can't promise to keep this visit platonic."

"Then my wishes may come true?"

Cyl swallowed hard. Why couldn't she just take Tawny to bed now? Why the pretense of poker? Still, it would up the anticipation factor for sure.

"I don't know where the cards are."

"I do."

Cyl followed Tawny down the hall to a spare room. Tawny opened a trunk and Cyl saw it was full of games. Tawny found a deck of cards and held them up.

"I have to warn you," she said. "I'm a bit of a card shark."

"I think I can hold my own."

"Good luck. High cut deals."

Tawny cut a king and Cyl a nine. Tawny would deal first. Tawny won the first two hands and Cyl dutifully removed her shoes and socks.

"Are you afraid of what I might see?" said Tawny.

"Making you work for it."

"I see."

Cyl won the next two hands which resulted in Tawny losing her sandals and her top. Her full breasts in plain view made it hard for Cyl to concentrate. She lost the next hand and took off her shirt. She knew her hard nipples were obvious under her wife-beater but didn't care. Tawny's nipples looked like they could cut glass.

Cyl won again and Tawny took off her shorts, revealing she was commando.

"Looks like I lost," Tawny said.

"Looks like I won."

Cyl stripped out of the rest of her clothes and pulled Tawny against her. She kissed her with such passion she thought she would bruise Tawny's lips. But Tawny kissed back with equal fervor.

"Damn," said Tawny. "You know how to kiss."

"You're about to experience what else I know how to do."

She lifted Tawny so she was sitting on the table. Cyl sat in the chair and spread Tawny's legs. Her pink wonderland was right in front of her and she admired it for a long time.

"Are you just going to look?" said Tawny.

"Patience, Tawny. You're beautiful. I can't help but stare at perfection."

Tawny placed her hand between her legs and lazily rubbed her clit.

"What do you think you're doing?" said Cyl.

"One of us has to enjoy this."

Cyl took Tawny's hand and sucked her fingers.

"You taste amazing," she said.

She buried her face between Tawny's thighs and coated herself with Tawny's juices. She smelled incredible and tasted even better.

Cyl slid her fingers inside Tawny and watched as Tawny threw her head back as she slid her hips forward to take Cyl deeper.

Cyl found Tawny's clit swollen and ready. Cyl licked it while she moved her fingers in and out. Tawny closed her thighs around Cyl's face as she cried out her pleasure.

Just warming up, Cyl eased Tawny down on her back. She continued to plunge deep inside her while she sucked on one then the other taut nipple. She loved how hard Tawny's tits were as she ran her tongue over them.

Tawny was mewling and Cyl knew she was close again.

"Tell me what you need," whispered Cyl.

"Keep doing what you're doing."

Cyl sucked harder and fucked her more intensely. Soon she felt Tawny clamp hard around her fingers as she screamed her release yet again.

Tawny lay back on the table, spent. Cyl straddled one of her legs as she sucked her nipples again.

"I've got no more," said Tawny.

"Okay. If you're sure?"

"I am. But you're so deliciously wet. Time for me to fuck your brains out."

Cyl helped Tawny off the table and climbed up. She spread her legs so wide her hips hurt, but she didn't care. She needed an orgasm desperately.

Tawny kissed her hard on her mouth while her fingers found Cyl's center.

"More," said Cyl. Tawny filled her and began moving in and out. Cyl arched her hips off the table to take every inch of Tawny.

Her mind went blank. All she could do was feel. And she felt fucking amazing. She was close to coming. So very close. All she needed…Tawny lowered her mouth and took Cyl in. The feel of Tawny's tongue on her clit was just what the doctor ordered. Cyl catapulted into orbit then softly sank back into her body.

"I suppose I should leave now?" Tawny said.

"You don't have to. You could stay the night." Cyl thought starting her day with a dose of Tawny wouldn't be a hardship.

"I appreciate that. But it would be too weird."

"Weird?"

"I wouldn't feel right sleeping in Marjorie's bed. I'm sorry."

"No. That's fine. I get that."

"Thanks for tonight, Cyl. I'll never forget it."

"It was a lot of fun, wasn't it?" Cyl said.

"Maybe we can do it again sometime? Don't worry. I'm not looking for a relationship. I just thought it might be fun to hook up once in a while."

"You know where to find me," said Cyl.

She walked Tawny to the door and made sure she got in her car safely. When Tawny's car was out of sight, Cyl closed the door and went to bed.

Cyl had weird dreams that night. Her parents were in them and were beating her with clubs and sticks and whatever they could get their hands on. Cyl woke in the morning feeling anything but rested.

She hadn't had those kinds of dreams in years. It must be all the talk about Aunt Marjorie bringing up even more loathing of her parents. They were real pieces of work. No doubt about it.

Cyl cleaned up the dining room and put the cards back in the trunk. She looked through the other games in there. Maybe she should invite some of Aunt Marjorie's friends over to play. Maybe. She'd see.

She finished her coffee and was outside cutting plywood to fit the holes in the lighthouse walls when she heard a car pull up. Luna got out. Cyl called out to her and Luna walked over.

"How are you this morning?" said Luna.

"Great. How are you?"

"Doing well. I was wondering if we could talk?"

"Um. Sure. Give me a second."

"No. You're busy. Let's meet for drinks this afternoon. Say three o'clock at the pub?"

"Sure. I'll be there."

"Great. See you then."

Cyl carried a piece of plywood up the stairs and smelled something odd. It was like smoke, but not exactly. Was it cigarettes?

No. It was sweeter. Cigar maybe? Or a pipe? Had someone been in the lighthouse? Was someone still there?

Gripping her hammer tightly, she set the plywood down and crept up the stairs. The smell got stronger. She got to the gallery and found it empty. The smell was strongest there, but there was no one there. Where had the smell come from?

She finished working on the walls at two, took a quick shower, then took an Uber to Ybor City. She got to the pub a few minutes early, ordered a Guinness, and watched sports while she waited for Luna.

Luna arrived at quarter after.

"Sorry I'm late," she said. "You'll find I'm horrible with making it on time. Absolutely horrible."

"That's okay. I had nothing else going on. Shall we get a table?"

"Yes."

Cyl waited for Luna to bring up why she needed to talk to her, but she didn't. Cyl grew frustrated but kept her voice calm.

"So what do we need to talk about?" Cyl said.

"As you know, your aunt and I were very close."

"Right."

"I have a television show. We haven't exactly talked about that yet."

"No. We haven't." Cyl thought Luna very attractive if not more than a little annoying.

"Your aunt was going to let me feature the lighthouse on it. I was wondering if you'd be interested."

"What kind of show?"

"We explore unexplained phenomena. I specialize in haunted places in or around Tampa."

"So why feature the lighthouse?" Cyl was growing more annoyed by the minute.

"Marjorie thought it was haunted."

"Seriously?"

"Yes. Are you a believer?"

"No."

"Oh," said Luna.

"Yeah. Like not at all. Maybe you can get whoever buys the place on your show, but not me. I'm not interested."

"You haven't noticed anything strange around there?"

"Not a thing. There's no such thing as ghosts."

"That's where you're wrong," Luna said. "There are such things and sometimes they're good and sometimes not. Marjorie was a big-time believer. That place is haunted."

"If I meet any ghosts, I'll call you."

"You're not taking me seriously."

"Not at all," said Cyl.

"And what did you mean about whoever buys the place? You're not keeping it?"

"Not a chance. I'm fixing it up and selling it."

"But Marjorie left it to you for a reason," said Luna. "She wanted you to have it. She wanted to keep it in the family."

"Look. I hear what you're saying. But I have a life in Fort Collins. I don't belong here in Tampa. It's not for me."

"You're a cold, heartless bitch. You're nothing like your aunt. I was wrong. We all were."

"I think this would be a good time for me to get home. You enjoy your life, Luna. And I'll enjoy mine."

"It really is that easy for you, isn't it?"

"It really is. Good-bye."

Chapter Six

Cyl wasn't feeling like working on the lighthouse. She decided to take in the sights and sounds of Tampa that weren't Ybor City. She found the Heights, the gayborhood of Tampa proper. She had breakfast and sipped coffee and checked out the tapestry of people who wandered the streets.

People watching wasn't holding her interest. She decided she needed some beach time. She drove to neighboring St. Petersburg, took off her shoes, and walked along the water. She was shocked at how warm the gulf was. She'd always assumed any ocean, sea, gulf, or bay would be freezing, but not the water there. It was therapeutic. She decided to dress more appropriately next time so she could actually swim.

After a couple of hours in the sun, she headed back to the cottage. She took a beer out of the fridge and headed up to the gallery in the lighthouse. She sat and gazed at the water and let herself relax and really see the beauty there. She didn't have anything she had to do and there were a lot of worse places she could have been.

She finished her beer and started toward the staircase when she kicked something. Shoeless, she let out a string of expletives, looked down, and saw her hammer. What the hell was it doing in the gallery? She was certain she had left it under the staircase with the rest of her tools.

Had someone been in the lighthouse? That thought was disconcerting. Then she remembered the smell of tobacco the week before. Someone was getting into the lighthouse at night. She grabbed her wallet and headed to the hardware store to buy a deadbolt.

Once that was installed, she felt much safer. She didn't know who'd been in the lighthouse. Probably just some kids since nothing appeared to have been stolen. But she didn't like the idea of anyone in there without her permission. She'd leave the door unlocked during the day if she was home, but at night it would be deadbolted.

The following day she was back at work on the lighthouse when her watch buzzed. Who would be texting her? She took her phone out of her pocket to see a text from Martinique.

Hey stranger. Just checking to see when you thought you'd be picking up the ashes.

Oh shit. I completely forgot. What day is today? Friday? Can I pick them up Monday?

Sure. Or we could meet somewhere tonight.

Say when and where.

With the details sorted Cyl turned her focus back to the paneling she was struggling with. She had cut the plywood several times, but no matter how obsessive she was with measuring, it never seemed to fit.

"Fuck it." She moved to another section. The panels were about half complete. Then she'd paint before she started on the cottage. The cottage wasn't in bad shape, but it definitely needed to be brought to the twenty-first century. She couldn't even guess how old the hot water heater was. And the air conditioning unit left much to be desired. She probably had another month in Tampa. Things were progressing nicely.

At five o'clock, she locked the lighthouse then had a beer while she fixed dinner. After dinner, it was time for a shower and then she was perplexed again as to what she should wear. She'd be inside a club, so ostensibly there would be air conditioning. But if there were a lot of people, it could still get hot.

She chose a pair of black chino shorts and a green golf shirt. She ran some gel through her hair to make it spiky, sprayed her cologne, and was greeting her Uber driver at nine o'clock. As she rode to the Pink Pearl, she wondered how the night would play out. Would she sleep with Martinique again? Or would she simply meet her and then be left to her own devices? Either way appealed tremendously.

The driver dropped her off and she could hear the music in the street. Or maybe that was music from one of the million other clubs that surrounded her. People were milling about on the street. Gay couples, lesbian couples, lost-looking straight couples. Everyone seemed to be enjoying themselves though and Cyl knew she was where she belonged.

She walked into the Pink Pearl and saw signs everywhere announcing in was Eighties Night. That could be fun. Cyl liked the oldies. She went to the bar to get a drink and found Martinique already there.

"You're early," said Cyl.

"As are you."

"Guilty as charged. What's good here?"

"I'm having a Sex on the Beach."

"Now that sounds fun," Cyl said. "But I think I'll just have a rum and Coke, please."

"No beer?"

"Not right now. I'll probably have one a little later. Depending on if I build up my thirst."

"You plan on dancing the night away?" said Martinique.

"I don't know. You're the one calling the shots. By the way, where is my aunt?"

"In my car. She's safe there."

"Okay. Thanks," said Cyl.

"Shall we get a table? Or a booth? Which do you prefer?"

Cyl checked out the dance area. There were several tables with tall stools along the outside of the dance floor. Then there were booths and up some steps on another layer were more booths.

"Let's get a booth on the main floor," she said.

"Lead the way."

Cyl found the last unoccupied booth and waited for Martinique to sit.

"We should sit together rather any across from each other," Martinique said. "So we can both watch the dancers."

"Sounds good. Scoot in."

Cyl draped her arm loosely over Martinique's shoulders. She didn't want to appear possessive but wanted Martinique to know she was interested. Just in case she wondered.

Within an hour the place had really filled up. There were women of all shapes and sizes shaking their things to songs from the eighties.

"Would you like to dance?" said Cyl.

"Sure."

They danced to "Girls Just Wanna Have Fun," but then "Tainted Love" came on and they couldn't decide if it was a slow song or not so they opted to get refills instead. After watching for a while, they got up and boogied with the rest for song after song.

Finally, Martinique leaned in and said, "I'm about at my limit. Can we get some air?"

Cyl nodded and followed Martinique to a courtyard behind the club. The oppressive heat and humidity hit her hard.

"Fuck," she said. "How can you live in this?"

Martinique laughed.

"Believe it or not, you get used to it."

"I choose not to believe that."

"You're a wuss," said Martinique.

"I'm not. I just don't like this weather."

"It's better than being on the crowded dance floor."

"If you say so."

"I do. So, how late did you want to stay? I should get going. It was a long week. I could drop the ashes off at the cottage any time."

"That's okay," said Cyl. "I'll get them now and head home. It has indeed been a long week."

As they walked along the avenue, Cyl told Martinique about the kids who'd been in her lighthouse.

"Did you actually see anyone?" said Martinique.

"No."

"Hm."

"What?"

"You know your aunt believed the place was haunted."

Cyl stopped and rolled her eyes.

"Not you, too."

"I'm just sayin'."

"Well, don't. I don't believe in ghosts and I don't think the lighthouse is haunted. I think some kids were getting in and getting their kicks. End of story."

"Suit yourself," Martinique said.

"Is everyone here crazy?"

"No. The area has a rich history. That's all I'll say."

"Fair enough."

They got to Martinique's car.

"Thanks for meeting me out tonight," said Cyl. "I do appreciate it."

"You're quite welcome. It was good for me to go dancing."

"Yeah. It was fun. We could do it again sometime."

"Maybe. I think you need to broaden your social horizons though. I can't always play tour guide."

"I know this. But we have fun together."

"That we do," Martinique said. "Okay. Here are the ashes. Let me know when you're going to spread them. I think I'd like to be there."

"Of course." Cyl took the urn.

"Good night, Cyl."

"Drive carefully."

When she got home, Cyl put the black urn on the shelf in the living room.

"I wish I could have known you when you were alive," she said. "Instead of hanging out with you now."

She thought of the task of spreading her aunt's ashes. She supposed she'd need to charter a plane to do it right. And now she had Tawny and Martinique to consider. She supposed she should reach out to crazy Luna, but that thought made her skin crawl. No. She'd get a four-seater and keep the party to a minimum.

Cyl woke the next morning later than normal. And she was still tired. She didn't use to feel this way after a night out. She reasoned it was the heat and humidity that had done her in and not the rum and Cokes.

She perused the bookshelves while she waited for her coffee. There were several about ghosts.

"You're not haunting me, are you, Aunt Marjorie?" She laughed, chose a book on Jose Gaspar, poured a cup of coffee, and sat down to read.

Jose Gaspar turned out to be a colorful character indeed. No wonder the people in Tampa were obsessed with him. He was a pirate, to be sure. But he had his redeeming qualities too. She made herself put the book down and get to work.

She unlocked the lighthouse door and heard a noise she was very familiar with. Her table saw was on. Why would she have left that on? Sure, she'd been in a hurry to meet Martinique, but leaving her tool on was unacceptable. She needed to be more careful.

Cyl turned it off and looked at the pile of plywood she still had to cut. She had no desire to do it. Any of it. But she had to make the place nice if she wanted to sell it. And she most definitely wanted to sell it.

She decided to paint what she'd already done. That would be different and fairly mindless. But, after an hour, she was feeling lightheaded. She stepped outside for some fresh air. God, but the weather sucked there. Literally. It sucked the air from her lungs, and it sucked her will to get anything done.

Still, she had to air out. She walked down to the rocky point just to see what it was like. The land was very narrow there and she took careful steps so as not to fall in. She wondered if Florida had sharks. She'd have to look that up.

The point stood high off the water and she wondered how many ships the lighthouse had saved over the years. It wouldn't have been pretty to run aground there. In fact, it would have been downright ugly.

Feeling better, she hiked back to the lighthouse, put the lid on the paint can, and took her tools out to wash. She locked the deadbolt behind her, washed her roller and brush, and went into the cottage for more reading.

She popped the top off a cold one and settled on the couch. She took out her phone and searched for sharks in Tampa and St. Petersburg. There were about a dozen species that popped up. Great. If the heat and humidity don't kill you, go relax in the gulf and the sharks would get you. She couldn't wait to get home.

CHAPTER SEVEN

The somber day dawned bright and beautiful. Cyl was awake at seven and took her coffee up to the gallery to admire the gulf and try to wrap her head around what the day would entail. Tawny and Martinique would arrive at ten. She tried to focus on the tangible rather than contemplate what she was being asked to do.

She told herself she was overreacting, being too emotional. She hadn't even known her aunt. But she felt like she had. After being there for a few weeks and hearing everyone's stories, she honestly felt like she was getting to know Aunt Marjorie, her mother's mysterious sister that her parents refused to mention in her presence.

Cyl felt like this was truly the end of something remarkable. Though Aunt Marjorie had been dead for a while. This wasn't the end. This was simply carrying out her aunt's wishes. And Cyl couldn't afford to be maudlin. She figured she'd need to be strong for Tawny and Martinique. They would surely be wrecks.

She took her shower and checked out her wardrobe. What did one wear on an occasion such as this? She put on her black skinny jeans and a black golf shirt. Somber and respectful. It would work.

Martinique arrived first wearing a long blue skirt with a yellow blouse. She looked comfortable, cheery. Tawny arrived wearing khaki shorts and a Hawaiian print shirt.

"You two look like you're partying or something."

"And you look like you're going to a funeral," said Martinique. "That ship has sailed. Let's consider this a celebration of Marjorie's life."

"Then I should change?"

"Need help?" Tawny and Martinique said together.

"Yes. Why don't you both come help me choose what I should wear."

She didn't miss the way Tawny and Martinique looked at each other, but she didn't have time for that right then. They had a plane to catch and she didn't want to be late.

"What's your favorite color?" said Tawny.

"Green."

"Okay. Then put on some shorts and a green T-shirt and let's get on the road."

"A T-shirt? Are you serious?" Cyl said.

"Dead," said Martinique. "Now change already."

While Cyl was changing she heard a commotion in the front of the house. Someone was yelling. What the hell was going on?

She found Luna had arrived and was raising holy hell about not having been invited.

"What exactly is your problem?" said Cyl.

"You're the one with the fucking problem. How dare you not ask me to go today? You knew how important it would be to me."

"Apparently, I didn't, or I would have asked." Cyl had been happy thinking Luna was out of her life for good. She was decidedly not happy to have her reappear.

"Liar."

"Luna, calm down. Let's talk this out civilly. Maybe you can go, too." Martinique looked at Cyl.

"It's only a four-seater. And the pilot needs one of those."

"We're going to have a celebration when we get back. Why not wait here for us?" said Tawny.

"This is so unfair." Luna broke down in tears. She was crying. Ugly crying. And Cyl had no idea what to say or do so she stood there feeling like an idiot.

"We kind of need to get going," she said. "Look. Why don't the three of you take Aunt Marjorie? I'll wait here until you get back."

"Are you sure?" said Martinique.

"Yeah. She didn't say I had to spread her ashes, did she? She just said she wanted them spread over the gulf. So one of you can take care of that."

"Thank you, Cyl." Luna hugged her. "This means so much to me."

"You're welcome. Now grab Aunt Marjorie and go before we have to reschedule."

Luna took Aunt Marjorie off the shelf and the others left, leaving Cyl feeling a strange combination of disappointed and relieved.

She kept herself busy getting the meat and cheese and vegetable trays set up. And making sure enough champagne was chilled. She made herself a bloody Mary and climbed to the gallery again to watch the plane fly by.

The plane flew low enough and slow enough that Cyl could see her aunt's ashes blowing in the wind. She wondered if crazy Luna would let her keep the urn. Not that it mattered in the big picture, but she'd gotten used to seeing it on her shelf and the shelf looked empty without it.

They returned with Tawny and Martinique seeming jubilant while Luna was uncharacteristically quiet.

"I guess I should leave now," Luna said.

"There's plenty of food and drink," said Cyl. "You're welcome to stay."

"You don't hate me?" Her eyes were pleading.

"Hate you? Hardly. By the way, where's the urn?"

"We left it in my car," said Martinique.

"Okay, well, I'd really like it back. So please don't leave without returning it."

"We won't."

"Thanks."

Cyl got the trays out of the refrigerator and set them on the dining room table.

"Who wants champagne?"

"Are we having mimosas?" said Luna.

"That could be arranged. Who wants champagne and who wants a mimosa?"

Drinks poured, they filled their plates and sat around the table.

"Do you guys ever go to the beaches around here?" Cyl said.

"Sure," said Martinique. "Davis Islands is our go-to. We're about due for a trip. Would you like to go?"

"What about the sharks? I've been reading there are lots of sharks in the area and this is the prime season for them."

"Well, we don't go out deep," Tawny said. "So we don't worry about them."

"Hm. Still…As much as I enjoyed the water at St. Pete's the day I went, I don't know if I could actually get in the water now."

"You went to St. Petersburg? By yourself? Why didn't you invite one of us?" said Luna.

"I don't know. I guess I needed some alone time."

"Fair enough."

"Okay so let's make a date now. When should we go to Davis Islands?" Tawny was clearly excited at the prospect.

"Next weekend," said Martinique. "Let's meet there Saturday at ten."

"You're coming, right, Cyl?" Luna said.

Cyl munched a broccoli floret while she pondered. Time with these lovelies and crazy Luna versus sharks. In the end hormones won out over common sense. Wasn't that always the case?

"Sure. I'll be there."

"Great." Tawny clapped.

"So how was it? Being up in the air? And how scary was it to drop her ashes?"

"It was amazing. Such a surreal experience," said Luna.

"It was beautiful," Tawny said. "Thank you so much for letting me be a part of that."

"It really was special. I'm glad we did that together," Martinique said. "Sorry you weren't with us, Cyl."

"That's okay. It made more sense for the three of you. After all, you knew her."

"Do you feel like you know her at all now? I mean, after your time here?" said Martinique.

"It's funny, but I do. I was just thinking the other night how I'm spending all this time with her while she's dead and how I wish I could have known her while she was alive."

"She would have loved you," said Tawny.

"Thanks."

The party went on into early evening when Luna announced she was ready for more than finger food.

"Let's go get some dinner. And then we should go dancing. The four of us."

"I'm up for it." Martinique glanced at Cyl. "You?"

"Sure. But we're calling a cab. None of us is driving at this point."

"Fair enough," said Tawny. "This is going to be so much fun."

They worked together to clean the dining room then called a taxi to take them to Ybor City. Martinique sat in the front while the other three crammed together in the back. Tawny was practically sitting on Cyl's lap. Not that Cyl minded. By the time they got to the restaurant, Tawny had been stroking Cyl's thigh for some time. This could prove to be a very interesting night indeed.

They each ate a solid dinner to soak up what they'd been drinking and to hopefully stop them from going overboard at the club. At least that was Cyl's way of looking at it.

The Pink Pearl was hoppin' when they arrived. It was wall-to-wall women and hotter than hell. Both temperature wise and eye candy wise. It was off the charts.

"I'll buy the first round." Cyl had to shout to be heard.

"Nonsense. You've done enough. I'll buy. Champagne for everyone?" said Luna.

"Actually, I think I'd like to switch to beer. Just a pale ale for me, please," Cyl said.

Luna returned with a bottle of champagne, three glasses, and a beer for Cyl. They moved closer to the dance floor. Martinique pointed to an empty booth upstairs and they hurried to get it before anyone else.

"That was lucky," said Tawny. "Something tells me this is going to be a very lucky night."

Cyl almost blushed when Tawny winked at her. How could she let Martinique know she'd slept with Tawny? And vice versa? Would they care? Hell, they probably already knew. Whatever. Cyl didn't plan on taking either of them home that night. She wasn't about to ruin any friendships to get laid.

Somehow, she ended up on the same side of the table as Luna. Not ideal. Safe, but not ideal. The others were on their second bottle of champagne and they had all danced to several songs. Everyone was festive and the others seemed to be feeling no pain.

"Wait, wait, wait," Luna yelled so the others could hear her. "I have a question."

"Shoot," said Tawny.

"Do y'all believe the lighthouse is haunted?"

Cyl leaned back against the booth. Hard. She couldn't believe they were going to have this conversation. It was the last thing she needed. Luna going on about the haunted lighthouse again.

"Of course," Tawny said. "Marjorie said it was and I believe Marjorie."

"I don't believe in ghosts," said Cyl.

"I don't know," Martinique said. "That's a tough question. I'm still not certain about the hereafter, but some strange things have happened there."

"Like what?" Cyl wanted to know what constituted a haunting.

"Like she could feel a presence. Marjorie was very in touch with the other side," said Luna.

"A presence? Look. I know some kids were getting in and messing with my stuff. But it hasn't happened since I deadbolted the door."

"Are you sure it was kids?" Tawny said.

"It had to be. They were moving my tools around and smoking in the gallery. Typical kid stuff."

"Ah!" Luna jumped in her seat. "So you've smelled the tobacco too?"

"What do you mean, 'too'?"

"Marjorie smelled tobacco on more than one occasion." Luna's eyes shone.

"So the kids got in there and smoked then, too. It doesn't say anything about it being haunted. Now, can we change the subject?"

They silently made their way to the courtyard. The music was muted there, but not by a whole lot. At least they didn't have to shout to be heard.

"So are you like a staunch disbeliever or just have no reason to believe yet?" Martinique said to Cyl.

"I thought we were changing the subject."

"Sorry. I was just curious."

"I do wonder if Marjorie will hang around. I wish you'd let me try to communicate with her," said Luna.

"You can try all you want. She's gone."

"You really wouldn't object?"

"Why would I? Do I think it's nonsense? Absolutely. Should that stop you from having your fun? No."

"We should have a séance," said Tawny.

"Let's not get carried away," Cyl said.

"It might be interesting," said Martinique.

"Oh, yes. Let's have a séance." Luna clapped. "Saturday night when we get home from the beach. It'll be awesome."

All three of them were staring expectantly at Cyl.

"What can it hurt?" she finally said. "Saturday night it is."

CHAPTER EIGHT

Cyl slept until eight the following Saturday. She was tired and owed it to herself. She woke up, pulled on the board shorts and muscle shirt she'd bought the day before and settled down to enjoy her coffee. She was actually really looking forward to a day at the beach. And there were worse women to hang out with.

The day should be a lot of fun. The night? Whatever. She decided to make a point of asking Luna what exactly made Aunt Marjorie think the lighthouse was haunted. Then, she would provide perfectly logical explanations and maybe, just maybe, the ridiculous séance would be canceled.

When she got to Davis Islands, there were several boats anchored near the shore. Cyl wondered if she'd be able to use her new boogie board. Or if she'd want to get in the water at all. She tried not to let it dampen her spirits. She grabbed the boogie board and set off in search of the rest of the group.

Martinique stood and waved so Cyl headed over to sit with her.

"Where are the others?" she said.

"Tawny is on her way and Luna? Well, Luna's always late."

"Got it. Are we going to be able to swim do you think? Because it's already too hot to just sit here."

"We'll be able to get in. No worries. Though you won't find any waves for that." Martinique pointed to the boogie board.

"That's too bad. But we're still going to have a good day."

"We are. How are you feeling about tonight?"

"Like it's a waste of time. But whatever. If that's what it takes to convince you guys the place isn't haunted, then so be it."

Martinique laughed.

"So skeptical. There's not a believing bone in that body, is there?"

"Not a one."

"I don't know. So much of Tampa is said to be haunted. Particularly in Ybor City. I can't help but wonder."

"I was going to ask Luna, but I'll ask you instead. What made Marjorie believe the lighthouse was haunted? And not the cottage? Only the lighthouse, right?"

"There were odd things," said Martinique. "The smell of tobacco. Cold air where it should have been hot. Things moved around or rearranged. Things that as you say you can attribute to someone being in the lighthouse. But the weirdest one was you know that round table as you enter the lighthouse? Well, she put fresh flowers there one day and the next day they were dead. Like wilted and brown. Very strange."

"Hm. That is odd. But someone could have poisoned them. But nothing weird happened in the cottage?"

"Not that I can remember."

"So what good is the séance in the cottage going to do?"

"I think Luna wants to have it in the lighthouse," Martinique said. "Just inside the front door."

"Interesting. Fine by me. I'm just here for the beer as they say."

Martinique laughed again.

"We'll see. I do appreciate you going along with it though."

"No harm, no foul."

"You two look so serious," Tawny said. "Am I interrupting anything?"

"Of course not," said Cyl. "We were just talking about tonight."

"Oh, yes. I'm so excited."

"I'm sure Luna will be, too. If she makes it." Cyl laughed.

"Luna's definitely on her own schedule. No clue about time management."

"So it would seem."

"Let's get in the water." Tawny had spread her towel on the other side of Martinique. "It's hot."

They splashed around in the shallow water, but Cyl needed more. She moved toward the boats and dove under. She came up and felt refreshed. She looked back to where she'd left Tawny and Martinique, but they were gone. She searched the shore and saw that Luna had arrived. And from a distance, Luna looked amazing. Her suit barely contained her large breasts and Cyl thought it was too bad she had a screw loose. She wouldn't mind a toss in the hay with Luna.

As she made her way back to the group, Cyl pondered if any of them were mentally sane. Even Martinique seemed to believe in ghosts. And Martinique had seemed to have a decent head on her shoulders. Tawny was a free spirit so she wasn't surprised at her, but Martinique really shocked her.

"Hi, Cyl!" Luna called to her as she hurried up the hot sand.

"Hi, Luna. Glad you could make it."

"I wouldn't have missed it."

Cyl struggled to keep her focus on Luna's eyes and not her huge breasts. She wanted to bury her face between them and suck and nibble and thoroughly enjoy them. She hadn't expected to ever have such a visceral response to Luna, but it was there. And she wasn't sure how to turn it off. Or if she wanted to.

They all lay back on their towels to relax and soak up rays. Cyl was growing bored and searched her mind for something to talk about.

"So I know Tawny's story," she said. "But Luna and Martinique, how did you meet my aunt?"

"I used to work for a firm," said Martinique. "They handled all Marjorie's affairs. I was assigned to your aunt and we hit it off. Soon she was inviting me over for coffee or game nights. We really clicked."

"I see," said Cyl. "So these game nights? They were pretty well known?"

"People would bring card tables and folding chairs," Tawny said. "The living room would be crammed with us. Not to mention the kitchen and the dining room. They were so much fun."

"If there were so many people at them, how is it I've only met you three?"

"Just lucky I guess." Martinique winked.

"I guess," said Cyl. "What about you, Luna?"

"I used to…well, sometimes I still do…volunteer at hospitals. Your aunt had had routine gallbladder surgery, but something went wrong. She ended up with an infection. I was one of a handful of people who could go visit her. This was twenty years ago. I would read to her, brush her hair, put lotion on her, you know. Little things that made her feel normal. It was only for a few days, but the bond we forged was strong. We've been tight ever since."

Cyl digested the information.

"Wow. Thank you for being there for her."

"It was my pleasure. I loved your aunt. As did so many others. She was a remarkable woman."

"I've been contemplating having an official celebration of life. So I could meet more people who knew her."

"That would be great," said Tawny.

"And completely against her wishes," said Martinique. "She specifically said she didn't want anything like that. 'Nothing so maudlin' is how she put it."

"Well then, there goes that idea," said Cyl. "I would never go against her wishes."

"Thank you."

"Let's get wet," said Luna.

They splashed each other and dove underwater and just overall enjoyed themselves in the warm waters of the gulf. Cyl thoroughly enjoyed watching the others frolic and was grateful she had three new friends. Were they friends? Or merely acquaintances? She was picky who she let into her life, but these three had really wormed their way in. Even crazy Luna. Not that it mattered. She'd be gone in a few months and these people would be a distant memory.

They dried off and Cyl was feeling the effects of the sun.

"I think I'm going to head out," she said. "I've had enough sun. I'll see you all tonight?"

"I'm famished," said Luna. "Would you like to grab some lunch?"

"All of us?" said Cyl.

"I'm not ready to leave," Martinique said.

"Nor am I. I'll be over tonight."

"Sounds good," said Cyl. "Let's go, Luna."

Luna had parked next to Mabel. They were talking about where to go for lunch.

"I'm not really dressed to go anywhere. Let's go back to the cottage. We can order in. I'll buy," said Luna.

"Sounds good. I'll see you there."

Cyl wasn't sure about the concept of spending a few hours alone with Luna. It could be nice, but Luna could be annoying as well. Still. She was a beautiful woman who had really been there for her aunt when she needed her, so she figured she'd give it a shot. Worst-case scenario, Cyl would plead the need to work to get rid of her if need be.

She needn't have worried. Luna came into the cottage wearing a sarong around her suit. Her tits on display were distracting to Cyl, but she did her best to calm her raging hormones.

"What would you like for lunch?" Luna said as she made herself comfortable on the couch.

"I don't care. How about a burger?"

"I know just the place."

Luna put her phone back in her purse.

"I feel like we may have turned the corner, don't you?" she said.

"How do you mean?"

"Well, when you left the pub, I felt like there was no hope for us to ever be friends. And now look at us."

Cyl nodded slowly.

"We don't necessarily see the world the same way. But you're a good person who was special to my aunt, so I can't write you off just like that."

"I appreciate that. I like you, Cyl. You're stubborn, hard-headed as they come, but you're also decent. I wish you weren't leaving. I'd love it if this lighthouse could stay in the family."

"How did my aunt come into this place? Do you know?"

"She inherited it. It's been in your family since it was built."

Cyl was shocked.

"Has it really? I had no idea."

"Have you ever traced your family tree?" said Luna.

"I haven't."

"Marjorie did. I'm sure her info is around here somewhere." Luna got up and looked over the bookshelf. "Ciara Murphy was the original keeper of the lighthouse."

"She's my ancestor?"

"Yes, she is. She met a tragic end, so her niece stepped up. And so on and so on until it got to you."

"Wow. That's pretty cool."

"So you can see why I really want you to keep it," said Luna.

"It's just not feasible."

"I get that. Do you have a niece or something who could take it over?"

"I don't. My niece doesn't know I exist."

"I'm sorry. That's tragic."

"It is," said Cyl. "But it can't be helped."

Their food arrived and they sat at the dining room table. Cyl was hungrier than she thought and she devoured her burger and fries.

"You want a beer or a glass of wine or anything?" she said.

"I'll have a glass of white wine if you have it."

"I have pinot grigio?"

"Perfect."

"You want to take it up to the gallery? We can look out over the gulf."

"Sure."

The gulf was like a lake. It was hot and still out there. But the view never ceased to amaze Cyl. It was beautiful.

"It's so peaceful up here," Cyl said.

"Mm. It's gorgeous. I could get used to this view."

"I often sip my coffee up here. It's a great way to start the day."

"I'm sure," said Luna. "I have to tell you. I've always had a fantasy about this place."

"How do you mean?"

"Never mind. I'm too embarrassed to say."

"Come on," Cyl laughed. "I need to know your fantasy."

"I've always thought it would be hot to have sex up here."

"Are you an exhibitionist?"

"Maybe," said Luna. "On some level. But no one could really see up here."

"True. But the wooden floor wouldn't be very comfortable." Although the prospect of taking Luna right then and there had Cyl's brain short-circuiting.

"I'm sure there are blankets around here. What's in that trunk over there?"

"I've never looked."

Cyl opened the trunk and found pillows and blankets.

"See?" said Luna. "I'm obviously not the only one who's had that fantasy."

"I could make that fantasy come true." The words were out before Cyl could stop them.

CHAPTER NINE

"Do you mean that, Cyl?"

"I don't know. I mean, why not? Let's spread the blankets and get you a pillow and I'll make it happen."

"You're not much of a romantic, are you?"

Cyl laughed. Then she allowed herself to brazenly look at Luna's breasts and then back at her eyes. She closed the distance between them and kissed her. Softly, almost chastely.

"That was nice," said Luna. "And, for the record, I like the way you look at me."

"And how's that?"

"Like a starving woman who needs me for nourishment."

"I like that." She kissed Luna again, a deeper, more passionate kiss while she pressed her body against Luna's breasts. They were soft yet firm and when Cyl stepped back, Luna's nipples were on full display.

"Oh, shit," said Luna. "I can't believe I'm going to say this, but I need you, Cyl. I need you now."

Cyl spread the blankets on the floor and eased Luna onto them. She lay next to her and kissed her again and ran her hands over her soft mounds, feeling her nipples poking her and needing more.

She fished a breast out of the swimsuit and tweaked the nipple. Then she bent and sucked the nipple in her mouth, taking a large portion of her breast with it. She tasted amazing and felt even better.

Luna was writhing against her. She held Cyl's head in place while she wrapped her legs around her hips. Cyl was a wet, throbbing mess, and it felt like Luna was too. Her suit left little to the imagination and Cyl felt her heat against her.

Cyl pulled the crotch of Luna's bathing suit to the side and stroked her with her fingers.

"Oh, God," said Luna. "Holy fuck, you feel good."

Cyl plunged her fingers deep into Luna's tight center with ease. She was slick with desire and Cyl met no resistance. She dragged her fingers out before slipping them in again as far as she could reach.

Luna bucked off the ground, urging Cyl deeper. She gyrated her hips to make sure Cyl was hitting all the right spots and Cyl was losing her mind at how hot it was.

She continued to move her fingers in and out as she moved lower so she could taste Luna's clit. It was swollen to the point of looking painful, so Cyl sucked on it expertly.

"Oh, yes," said Luna. "Oh dear God, yes. I'm going to come, Cyl. Oh crap. I can't hold out any longer. Oh, shit. That's it. Don't stop."

She screamed then and Cyl still didn't stop. She continued doing exactly what she was and Luna cried out again. Cyl climbed up next to Luna and kissed her, sharing her flavor with her.

"Damn, Cyl. That was hot. And totally unexpected."

"Mm. It was fun, though."

"Get out of those trunks so I can return the favor," said Luna.

Luna proved to have talented fingers and Cyl was soon gripping the blankets as release teetered just out of reach. Luna was in her and on her, probing deep then stroking her lips, her clit, and everything else she could find. She turned her attention to Cyl's clit and Cyl called Luna's name at the top of her lungs.

"Not a bad way to spend the afternoon," said Cyl.

"Not at all. Thank you, Cyl. You blew my fantasy out of the water."

"Always happy to help."

"I'll have to come up with some more fantasies."

"Works for me. Now, come on. The others will be here soon. We should clean up."

"Can we shower together?"

"Sure. Let's keep the fun going."

"I need to go out to my car and get my clothes. I'll join you in a minute."

The sight of Luna without clothes sent Cyl's libido skyrocketing anew. She lathered her hands and rubbed them all over Luna's ample chest and backside, then slipped them inside her. Luna turned around and braced herself against the wall and spread her legs. Cyl entered her from behind and wondered if she'd ever gotten that deep inside a woman before. She slid another finger in and wondered if Luna would be able to take her fist just as Luna cried out and collapsed back against her.

"I think I can trust my legs now," said Luna, "Though I have to say I'm enjoying your arms wrapped around me."

Cyl nibbled on Luna's neck.

"Oh no you don't," said Luna. "It's your turn now, lovergirl."

Luna dropped to a knee and took Cyl in her mouth. She licked and sucked and sucked and licked some more. Cyl was lightheaded. She leaned back against the wall and braced herself for the grand finale. She wasn't disappointed. Her whole body tensed, then white heat coursed through her limbs until she was finally coherent again.

They dried, dressed, and Cyl helped Luna set up in the lighthouse.

"I have a table," Cyl said. "My dining room table would have worked."

"Sorry. It needs to be a round table. Which is why I brought mine. Now, hand me the candles, please."

Cyl grabbed a couple of pillar candles and handed them to Luna.

"I need all six, please."

"You got it."

"Okay. Now we wait until the others get here. I'll need to heat some soup and we'll need to set out a glass of wine. That's what Marjorie always drank. I brought her favorite brand."

"You really think this is going to work? You think Marjorie is hanging around?"

"I'd like to think so. I'd be comforted if she was."

"I get that," said Cyl. "I totally get that."

"You're still not a believer, though."

"Let's just see how the night goes."

"Fair enough."

"Let's have a drink." Cyl knew she could use one. She took Luna's hand and guided her back to the cottage. She poured Luna another glass of wine while she popped the top of another beer.

They settled on the couch looking over a book about pirates in the Gulf of Mexico. It was nice. Cyl was learning and Luna wasn't annoying. Maybe Cyl had been too quick to judge her. Maybe.

There was a knock on the door and Cyl opened it to see a red-faced Tawny and a bronze Martinique standing there.

"Looks like you two stayed at the beach the whole day," said Cyl. She gently poked Tawny's forehead. "And looks like someone forgot their sunscreen."

"I forgot to reapply a couple of times. I'll be fine though."

"Great. Well, come on in. We're having drinks before the séance."

"Sounds wonderful," said Martinique. "I know I could go for a glass of wine."

"Me, too," said Tawny.

Cyl poured drinks and they sat around the dining room table visiting until Tawny said she couldn't take the suspense any longer.

"Let's do the séance," she said. "I've never been to one and I'm like a little kid at Christmas."

"Don't get your hopes up," Cyl said.

"I'm glad you're keeping an open mind, Tawny," said Luna with a pointed look at Cyl.

Cyl grinned and said to the group, "I understand we need to get ready? What do we need?"

"I'll heat up the soup," said Luna.

"We have to eat soup?" Cyl didn't feel like soup on this hot night in Tampa.

"It's not for us silly." Luna swatted Cyl's arm playfully. "It's for Marjorie. We have to have a warm offering for the spirit."

"And what flavor of soup do you think my aunt would like?"

"I picked up her favorite Italian wedding soup from a deli she loved."

Cyl had no witty comeback. Luna obviously had cared deeply and paid close attention to Aunt Marjorie's tastes. Cyl was duly impressed.

"Martinique? Will you open the bottle of Montepulciano?" said Luna.

"Oh," said Tawny. "That was her favorite."

They carried the soup and glass of wine to the lighthouse then went back to the cottage to get their own drinks.

"We won't really be able to drink," explained Luna. "We'll be holding hands. But if y'all would feel better with your drinks there, bring them."

They sipped their drinks while Luna lit the candles. Then Cyl turned off the lights and sat with the others. She was holding Luna's and Martinique's hands and felt like that way she would know if Luna tried to pull something. She didn't have faith, obviously, but also didn't trust Luna not to try to stage something. If she did, Cyl would be ready.

"Okay," said Luna. "It's time to read the words in front of you."

"I can't read in the dark," said Cyl.

"We've been practicing. Just do your best to do it from memory."

Luna and Martinique said, "Our beloved Marjorie, we bring you gifts from life into death. Commune with us, Marjorie, and move among us."

They sat silently for what seemed an eternity. Finally, Cyl grabbed her beer.

"She's not here." She omitted the "told you so," but it was implied.

"Don't break the chain," Luna said. "Let's try again."

Cyl set her beer down and grabbed hands again. The group repeated the calling to Marjorie to join them.

Cyl was about to grab her beer when the lights came on and went off again.

"What the hell was that?"

"Are you Marjorie?" said Luna.

"Can they talk?" said Cyl.

"Knock once on the table if you're Marjorie. Twice if you're not."

Cyl looked at each of them to make sure no one tried anything funny. Someone knocked twice.

"Are you the ghost who haunts the lighthouse?" One knock.

Cyl felt the goose bumps rising on her arms. This was trippy. She had to admit, it wasn't at all what she expected.

"We brought you food and wine," said Luna.

The wineglass sailed across the entryway and shattered against the wall.

"Would you like something to drink?" Luna went on. One knock.

The women all looked at each other obviously as unsure on how to proceed as Cyl was. While Cyl sat there, her beer bottle floated on the air to her right. When it came back to rest, it was empty.

"Shit," she whispered.

"Are you friendly?" said Tawny. One knock.

"Are you the one who keeps messing with my things?" said Cyl. One knock.

Cyl glanced over at Luna who grinned and winked at her. This was crazy. How could it be happening? She was about to break the circle when Martinique finally spoke.

"Do you know Marjorie?" One knock.

"Is she at peace?" Luna said. One knock.

"Thank you for joining us. You can go in peace," said Luna. Two knocks.

"You don't want this to end? What if we take a break and come back in a few?" One knock.

"Okay then. We'll be back. Let's break the circle now."

Cyl flipped the lights on and hurried to the cottage. The others joined her at a more leisurely pace. She poured herself a shot of bourbon and downed it. She wanted to down a few more but stopped herself. She poured two fingers in a glass and stood sipping it, trying to wrap her head around what she'd just witnessed.

Tawny seemed like she was about to burst.

"Can you even believe what just happened? So the lighthouse is haunted. And we've made contact with the ghost! It's so exciting," she said.

Martinique crossed to Cyl in the kitchen.

"How are you doing?"

"I don't know."

"I feel the same."

"I mean…was that real? Did that really happen?"

"We all experienced whatever it was," said Martinique.

Luna approached them and Cyl braced herself for the gloating.

"You okay?" she said.

"I will be."

"That was a lot," said Luna. "It shook me to the core. And I'm a believer. I can only imagine how you must be feeling."

"I don't know how to feel right now. I just…I don't know."

"I'm here. We all are. I think we should talk about it. As a group. Let's sit at your dining table and go over it. One question though. Are you willing to go back in there again tonight?"

CHAPTER TEN

Cyl pondered for a few minutes. Could she? Did she believe what she'd just witnessed?

"Let's sit at the table like you suggested," she said.

They all sat down and looked at each other.

"I'll start," said Luna. "What did we learn?"

"That the lighthouse is in fact haunted," said Tawny.

"So it would seem," said Martinique. "We also learned the ghost doesn't like wine, but seems okay with beer."

Cyl raised her glass.

"Nailed it," she said.

"Okay. Did we learn anything else?"

"Supposedly the ghost isn't malevolent," said Martinique. "Though who can be sure?"

"Why would the ghost lie to us?" said Luna.

"Why not?" said Cyl.

"I feel like it was a friendly ghost," Tawny said. "And I think it enjoyed our company."

"So did I," said Luna. "I'd like to get back in there and see what happens."

"Luna. This is a lot for someone like Cyl to handle. I wasn't a staunch non-believer and I'm reeling," Martinique said. "Let's take a few more minutes."

Luna placed her hand on Cyl's forearm.

"Seriously, Cyl. How are you?"

Cyl looked into the deep pools of brown that were Luna's eyes. There was no hint of gloating or amusement. She really wanted to know how Cyl was.

"I'm shaken. Shaken to my core. I don't know what the hell happened in there, but it was a hell of a lot more than I expected. I thought we'd sit there until you guys got bored and then we'd come back here and drink. That's most definitely not what happened."

"I want to know more about her," said Tawny.

"Why do you think it's female?" said Cyl.

Tawny shrugged.

"I don't know. Just the feeling I got."

"I'd like to know more, too," said Luna. "But I want to make sure Cyl's okay. And Martinique for that matter."

"Look," Cyl said. "Something was in the lighthouse. We all have to agree with that. But if it's capable of shattering wine glasses and drinking beer, what else is it capable of? How safe are we? Really?"

"I agree with Cyl," Martinique said. "I'm not convinced we won't be in danger if we go back."

"I'm afraid we will be if we don't," said Luna. "Maybe not all of us, but Cyl potentially."

"Fine," said Cyl. "Let's go back. I hear what Luna is saying, and I don't want any issues with Casper, friendly or not. But I'm not sacrificing another beer. I'll bring some rum that Marjorie had here. I won't drink it."

"Fair enough. Martinique, are you okay?"

"I'm terrified to go back in there, to be honest. I need more time to process. I think I'm going to head home."

"Fair enough," Luna said again. "I get that."

"I'll see y'all later." Martinique let herself out into the night.

"You both ready then?" Luna said.

"Let me get the rum."

They went back to the lighthouse, turned off the light, held hands, and summoned the spirit again. It responded almost immediately by knocking once on the table.

"We brought you some rum this time," Cyl said. One knock.

"Were you a woman?" Tawny said. One knock.

"Did you live here in Tampa?" Cyl looked at Luna like she'd asked a stupid question. But then came two knocks. She hadn't lived in Tampa? So why was she haunting this lighthouse?

Cyl noticed the glass of rum wasn't as full as it had been.

"Is rum your drink?" One knock.

"Did you die in Tampa?" asked Luna. Two knocks.

"Why are you here then? Why this lighthouse?" Cyl needed to know.

There were no knocks and Cyl realized she had to ask yes-or-no questions. How could they get to the bottom of this with yes-or-no questions only?

"Do you mean me any harm?" Cyl said. Two knocks.

"Did you hurt Marjorie?" Tawny said. Two knocks. Two very hard knocks.

"Were you married?" Cyl thought Luna asked the most bizarre questions. Two soft knocks.

"Did you have a lover?" Tawny said. One knock.

"Were you alive last century?" Cyl thought they should get to the bottom of where this ghost had come from and when. Not delve into her private life. Two knocks.

"The century before?" said Cyl. Two more knocks.

"The seventeen hundreds?" Luna said. One knock.

"Wow. So you've been around for a while," said Cyl. "Have you spent most of your time here?" One knock.

"Your knocks are getting weaker," said Luna. "Are you bored with us?" Two knocks.

"Are you getting weaker?" said Tawny. One knock.

"We can let you go. And come back another time," said Cyl. One knock.

"Thank you for joining us. You may go in peace."

They broke the circle and Tawny got the lights.

"Wow," she said. "That was amazing."

"It really was," said Luna. "Absolutely outstanding."

They cleared the table and went back to the cottage.

"I hate to do this. I'm so pumped I doubt I'll sleep, but I have to work at the bookstore tomorrow. I'd better say good night."

She hugged Luna then Cyl and let herself out.

"So tell me your thoughts," said Luna.

"I have to hand it to you," Cyl said. "You haven't gloated or said, 'I told you so' at all. You've been remarkably decent about this."

"I had nothing to prove, really. I had my beliefs but couldn't be sure. I'm just glad you were with us. I would be so frustrated trying to get you to believe what happened."

Cyl snickered.

"It would have been near impossible to convince me. I'm glad I was there too. I wish we could figure out who she is. Or was, as the case may be."

"Okay. I suppose I should get going," said Luna. "You going to be okay?"

"I guess. I kind of need to be alone with my thoughts. But then I sure as hell don't want to be alone with my thoughts."

"Pour me another glass. We'll hash this out until you're comfortable."

Cyl placed the wine in front of Luna then sat with her beer.

"I don't know. Like, I was so certain. As in, there was no doubt. I mean at all. It would be like finding out something like the moon landing wasn't real. Something you've accepted as fact all your life."

"I get that," said Luna. "I mean, I really do understand how earth-shattering this must be. I honestly do."

Cyl nodded.

"I appreciate that."

Luna patted her hand then gave it a gentle squeeze.

"Would you mind if I checked out the bookshelf? To see what books on ghosts she has?"

"I'll join you," Cyl said.

They each chose a book and read about famous and not so famous hauntings in Tampa.

"There's a lot of stuff about Ybor City," said Cyl. "I guess Martinique knew what she was talking about."

"No doubt. Ybor City is known for its ghosts. Lots of deaths in the cigar factories."

"I suppose that makes sense."

They refilled their drinks many times and kept reading. Finally, Cyl could barely keep her eyes open. She checked out the clock on the wall. It was after three.

"I'm going to have to call it quits," she said.

"Oh wow. Look at the time. I'd better call an Uber."

"You can stay here. Either with me or in the guest room. Wherever you'd be more comfortable."

"I can sleep with you, but I'm too tired for funny business."

"I agree."

When Cyl woke the next morning, she rolled over to see Luna watching her.

"Did you sleep at all?" Cyl said.

"I did. I slept hard. I just woke up."

"So were there any rules about funny business in the morning?"

"I do like the way you think."

They stripped and lay together. The feel of Luna's soft body against her drove Cyl crazy with desire. She kissed her way to Luna's huge breast and took as much of it in her mouth as she could.

"Damn, you make me feel good," said Luna.

"Mm."

The sound of the doorbell was like a bucket of ice.

"Shit," said Cyl. "Who could that be?"

Whoever it was rang the bell again.

"Fuck me. I'll go see who it is. You'd better get dressed."

Cyl opened the door to find Martinique standing there.

"I was coming over to check on you, but from the looks of things, you're doing just fine. Although honestly, you look like hell."

"Rough night."

"Long night," said Luna. "We must have gone through every book on ghosts that Marjorie owned."

"Seriously?"

"Afraid so. We were at it until after three. So, yeah. We're a little rough. Come on in. I'll get the coffee going."

"What did you find?"

"A bunch of interesting stuff, but nothing that applies to us really."

"That's too bad," said Martinique.

"Yeah. Ybor City though. Wow," said Cyl.

"Right? I told you."

"That you did. I think we should take a ghost tour or something."

"So now you're a believer?" Martinique said.

"Aren't you?"

Martinique took the piping hot cup of coffee.

"I suppose I am. I'm just glad you're okay. I mean, I know it shook your belief system."

"To my very core. But I can't deny what I witnessed, can I?"

"I suppose not. Although I half expected to show up here today and you have a logical explanation all worked out."

Cyl laughed.

"Maybe the old Cyl would have. The new Cyl is fascinated."

"I didn't realize there was an old and a new version," said Martinique.

"I think there is. I truly believe I've changed since I've been here. For the better. I think my aunt is watching out for me. Guiding me, if you will."

"I'm sure she is," Luna said.

"So you really mean to tell me, Casanova, that you and my friend Luna here only slept last night?"

"It was this morning and I swear. Are you jealous?"

"I'm not the jealous kind. I was just trying to wrap my brain around you and Luna. Though I've heard opposites attract."

"There was no funny business last night at all. We shared a bed, but only slept," Luna said.

"Okay. Enough about that. When are we going to visit with the ghost again? I'm really curious about it."

"Yeah. Me, too," said Cyl. "And is there a way to make it talk? I'm past asking yes-or-no questions."

"We could take a paper and pen," Luna said. "Maybe she'll write answers."

"Maybe," Martinique said. "But when?"

"I don't know. I'd say let's do it tonight, but I know you have to work tomorrow. As do I."

"We could do it early," said Martinique.

"It really should be dark."

"That's unfortunate."

"Yeah."

"So next Saturday then? Or Friday even?" Cyl said.

"Friday," said Martinique.

"Friday will be good. I hope Tawny can make it."

"Well, since I know you're okay, I guess I can take off," Martinique said.

"Me, too," said Luna. "You want to grab some breakfast, Martinique?"

"What am I? Chopped liver?" said Cyl.

"You need to go back to bed," said Luna. "Get some more sleep. We'll be in touch."

"I'm not going to argue with that."

Cyl slept but not peacefully. She had dreams about ghosts and other creatures of the night. They weren't benevolent creatures either. She woke from the nightmares drenched in sweat. She often had nightmares but could always shake them off as not real. Now she wasn't so sure.

She pulled on her board shorts and muscle shirt, grabbed her boogie board, and headed to St. Petersburg. Not that she needed more sun, but she thought boogie boarding would help release some of the pent-up energy. Energy she didn't get to expend with Luna that morning. That would have been a wonderful start to the day.

Who knew? She now believed in ghosts and was attracted to crazy Luna. Things were changing fast for her. All she could do was hold on and enjoy the ride.

CHAPTER ELEVEN

The following Friday night, Martinique, Luna, and Cyl waited as patiently as they could for Tawny to get off work and join them. They wanted to get the séance started. With pen and paper, Cyl was hopeful they'd learn more about her ethereal guest.

It was almost eleven when Tawny arrived, and they all went back to the lighthouse with rum, candles, pen, and paper.

"Do you think she can write?" Tawny said.

"We can only hope," said Cyl.

"It's rare that spirits can hold objects," said Luna. "But she definitely held Cyl's beer last week."

"That's true," Tawny said. "Oh, I hope she can write. I want to learn more about her."

"You're awfully quiet," Cyl said to Martinique.

"I'm just taking it all in."

"Okay. As long as there's nothing bothering you."

"Not a thing." Martinique smiled. "I'm rather enjoying myself."

They turned off the light, held hands around the table, and began to call the spirit.

After fifteen minutes, there was a knock on the table.

"Spirit!" Luna said. "You're here." Another knock.

"Do you know how to write?" Cyl said. One knock.

"We brought a pen and paper. Will you please write your name?"

They held their collective breath as the pen floated then touched the paper.

Brigid.

"Brigid? That's a great name," said Tawny.

"And you didn't die here?" Luna said. Two knocks.

"Where did you die?" said Cyl.

Sea.

"You were shipwrecked?" said Luna. One knock.

"Were you a merchant's wife?" Martinique said. Two loud knocks.

Pirate.

"No shit?" said Cyl. "That's too cool."

"Wait," said Martinique. "Were you a pirate? Or were you married to one?"

Me.

"Damn." Cyl had a newfound admiration for the once annoying spirit.

"Why are you here?" Luna said. Two knocks.

"You don't want to tell us?" Cyl couldn't hide her disappointment.

The pen floated then touched the paper again.

Aurnia.

"Aurnia? Is that a person?"

Lover.

"Your lover?" said Luna. One knock, but it was weak.

"Are you getting tired?" Cyl said. One knock.

"Is it hard to hold the pen?" Luna said. One knock. "Okay. Well, with the information you've given us, we should be able to ask you more yes and no questions. May we come back tomorrow?"

One knock and that was the last they heard from Brigid that night. They cleaned up the table and went back to the cottage. All four headed for the books.

"There's got to be a book on shipwrecks among all these," said Cyl.

"Yeah, but what are the chances we find hers?" Tawny said.

"Who knows? How many pirates were named Brigid? Between shipwrecks and pirates, we should be able to find something."

They scoured the books they could find until Martinique and Tawny announced they had to get some sleep.

"We'll see y'all tomorrow night, though, right?"

"Of course," said Tawny.

"Wouldn't miss it," Martinique said.

"We should go to bed," said Luna.

"Oh. You're staying over?"

"Is that okay?"

"Sure. That's fine. Are we sleeping? Or?"

"That, stud, is entirely up to you."

"In that case, let's go to bed now," said Cyl.

Cyl had been ready to doze on the couch but was suddenly wide-awake, hormones raging. She pulled Luna to her and kissed her hard on her mouth. Their tongues met and Cyl's center clenched. Damn, Luna had a strange effect on her.

Luna took a step back.

"We need to talk."

"Oh, shit. That wasn't on my agenda."

"I know." Luna laughed. She sat on the bed and patted the spot next to her. "Look, Cyl, I know we got off to a rocky start. But you've really grown on me. I want you to know it means something to me when we sleep together. I'm not asking you to say the same, I'm just letting you know how I feel."

"I've got to admit, I feel a connection with you, Luna. Crazy and unlikely as it is. So, let's kind of see where this goes, okay?"

"That would be wonderful."

She lay back and pulled Cyl on top of her. Cyl's knee found Luna's hot, wet center and she shuddered. Damn, Luna was so much fun.

Cyl made short order of Luna's clothes then took her own off. When they were skin-to-skin, Cyl thought her head would explode. Her blood rushed in her ears and she wanted to take Luna all at once.

She slid her hand between them and slipped her fingers inside while she suckled on a nipple. Luna writhed on the bed while her hand rubbed Cyl's back. Luna finally seemed to gain some semblance of control because her hands found Cyl's chest and tweaked her nipples.

The sensations were overwhelming for Cyl. Luna's tightness gripping her fingers, the swollen nipple in her mouth, and her own nipples being teased to infinity had her struggling to maintain.

Regretting moving away from Luna's hands, Cyl moved lower so she could take Luna in her mouth. Luna's rich flavor washed over her and she lost herself in pleasing her. She plunged her fingers deep again and again while focusing her tongue on Luna's clit. In no time Luna was screaming Cyl's name before collapsing on the bed.

Cyl coated Luna's breasts with her essence and cleaned them with her tongue.

"No more," Luna said. "It's your turn now."

Luna's tongue felt amazing on Cyl's clit, and it wasn't long before Cyl squeezed her eyes tight and watched the lights explode as she rode her climax.

The next morning, Cyl woke up needing Luna again. Luna was like a drug that Cyl needed to survive. It was an unfamiliar feeling for her, but one she didn't shy away from.

She took her every way she could. She used fingers, tongue, and fingers again and still she didn't get enough. Finally Luna lay back and laughed.

"Enough already. I'm sure I'll need to walk sometime today."

"Walking is overrated."

"So says you. You ready for your turn?"

"I'm good," said Cyl. "I'll make coffee."

They spent the day on Cyl's MacBook, searching for shipwrecks with a pirate named Brigid. They had no luck.

"Maybe the library will have something," Luna said. "They have volumes on pirates in the area."

"But we know she wasn't from the area. Her ship crashed at sea, remember?"

"Maybe we should search for Aurnia. Maybe we can learn about her?"

"Sure. Why not?"

Their search turned up a few interesting tidbits. There had been several Aurnias in the Tampa area. One promising one was Aurnia Byrne who had been in the Tampa area in the late sixteen hundreds.

"That's probably her," said Luna. "That's about when pirates in this area really flourished."

"Great. We'll ask Brigid tonight."

"Let's go get some dinner before the others get here," Luna said. "I'm famished."

"Sounds good to me. What are you in the mood for?"

"Besides you? Food." She laughed.

"I want a steak so steer me to the best steak restaurant."

"Oh, you're in for a treat."

After dinner, they stopped by a liquor store to pick up wine and beer and rum. It was eight o'clock by the time they got back to the cottage and found Martinique waiting for them.

"Come in out of this heat," said Luna.

"Is this your house too now?" Martinique raised an eyebrow at Cyl.

"We were out picking up supplies," Luna said. "Now come on in."

"I'd kill for a glass of wine," said Martinique. "By the way, Tawny can't be here tonight."

"No? That's too bad," said Cyl.

"Yeah. Her sister was in a car wreck so Tawny is helping with the kids."

"Is her sister okay?" Luna said.

"She's got a broken leg and a fractured arm, so she can't do much."

"That's horrible," said Cyl.

The three of them sat with their drinks at the dining room table and waited for it to get dark.

"Look what we found today." Cyl opened her MacBook and pushed it in front of Martinique.

"What am I looking at?"

"Aurnia Byrne. We think that was Brigid's lover."

"And why do we think that?"

"Well, we figured Aurnia had to have something to do with this area or Brigid wouldn't be haunting it," Luna said. "Of the three Aurnias we found, Aurnia Bynre was alive during the Golden Age of pirates. We'll ask Brigid tonight, of course."

"That's really fascinating," Martinique said. "Not as fascinating as the fact that you were here apparently all day researching with Cyl."

Luna blushed a deep crimson and Cyl exhaled heavily.

"I think Luna and I are going to try to make a go of things," she said.

"Is that right? Well, I wish you both the best of luck."

"Thanks."

It was finally dark enough to set things up in the lighthouse. Once the lights were off, they summoned Brigid. It took a half hour, but Brigid finally knocked on the table.

"Welcome, Brigid. Thank you for coming to meet us tonight."

Cyl and Martinique looked at Luna, who had seemed to take over the role of the medium. Which made sense to Cyl.

"We have more questions for you if that's okay?" Luna said. One knock.

"Was Aurnia's last name Byrne?" said Cyl. One knock.

"Wow," said Martinique.

"Was she one of your captives?" Luna said. Two knocks.

"How did you meet her?" Martinique said.

The pen hovered, dropped, hovered again.

Nurse.

"She cared for you after your wreck?" One knock.

"If you were wrecked at sea, how come you haunt my lighthouse?" Two knocks. "You don't want to answer that? Okay."

"Are you looking for Aurnia?" Luna said. One knock.

"Would you like us to help you?" said Cyl. There was no response. "Did I say something wrong?"

Two knocks.

"You don't want us to help you find Aurnia?" said Luna. There was no response.

"Sorry if I pissed her off," Cyl said. "I was just trying to be friendly."

"Maybe she's just tired," said Martinique. "Maybe we should let her go for the night."

Two knocks.

The pen floated again then touched the paper.

Help.

"You do want us to help?" Cyl was so excited she thought she could pee her pants. One knock.

"Excellent. We'll start tomorrow."

"Do you have any idea where to look?" said Martinique.

"If she did, she probably wouldn't be hanging around here," said Cyl.

"Unless she's buried around here."

"No." Cyl wasn't going to entertain that notion. "I'm sure she's not."

"You don't know that," Luna said. "It's very possible."

"Well then, why doesn't her ghost find Brigid and run off together?"

"It's not necessarily that easy."

"It's not necessarily that hard," said Cyl.

"As entertaining as it is to witness your first fight, shouldn't we focus more on Brigid?" said Martinique.

Cyl noticed the glass of rum was empty. She poured more.

"Do you want to be left alone now?" Two knocks.

"Okay. What was the name of your ship?" Luna said.

Tainted Rose.

"Nice," said Cyl. "I like that."

The chilly air that accompanied Brigid turned warm for a moment. Just a moment, but Cyl wondered if she'd made Brigid happy for at least a small bit of time.

"I haven't noticed any mischief this week," Cyl went on. "Are you through moving things around and stuff?" Two knocks. "Fair enough."

They all laughed and the air got warm again briefly. Cyl decided that was Brigid enjoying herself. And that made her happy.

The pen hovered and Cyl wondered if Brigid was going to start offering information rather than making them play a never-ending game of twenty questions.

Bye.

"You're leaving us? Do you want us to come back next week?"

One knock.

"See ya then," said Cyl.

"Good night, Brigid," Martinique said.

They went back to the cottage. It was late again, but Martinique didn't show any signs of leaving and Cyl was way too pumped to go to bed. Even with Luna.

"I think you should stay in the guest room tonight," Luna said to Martinique. "Then tomorrow we can all go to the library to look up gravesites."

"That's a great idea," said Cyl.

"Let's start looking them up on your computer now," Martinique said. "Though I'll have more wine because the invitation to stay sounds wonderful."

CHAPTER TWELVE

Sunday was spent perusing the library files for any information on Brigid or Aurnia.

"I can't believe we haven't asked Brigid her last name yet," said Martinique.

"No kidding," Cyl said. "Okay, we've searched shipwrecks and land titles and there's no info on Brigid or Aurnia Byrne. Maybe Byrne was a married name. Can we search marriage licenses?"

"Now you're talking," said Luna. "Let's see what we can find."

"I've got it," Martinique said hours later. "Aurnia Gallagher married Cormac Byrne. They got married in seventeen twelve."

"Too cool." Cyl forgot to keep her voice down and got a dirty look from another patron. "That's awesome. So now we look up land titles for Cormac Byrne."

"Another time," said Martinique. "I don't know about you two, but I'm fried."

"I'm getting a little crispy myself," Cyl said. "I can come back tomorrow."

"I'll see if I can join you," said Luna. "I have no idea what my schedule looks like tomorrow."

"It's all good. If you can get away, you know where to find me."

"I won't be free again this week. Nights I can get away though, so if we want to talk to Brigid, let me know."

"I think it's best we let her rest," Luna said.

"I have to say, she's been less mischievous since we've started draining her energy with séances."

"Is that right?" Martinique laughed.

"Yeah. Nothing was out of place this week."

"Amazing," Luna said.

"It is."

Martinique drove them back to the cottage, said good night, and promised to see them Friday night.

"You going home, too?" Cyl said to Luna.

"I really should."

"I could treat you to dinner first."

"You know how to impress, don't you?"

Cyl winked at Luna.

"I aim to please."

"Are we ordering or going out?" said Luna.

"Which would you prefer?"

"While I do love a nice restaurant, I'm fried from today. Let's order in."

They snuggled on the couch while they waited for their dinner.

"How's the lighthouse coming along?" Luna said.

"I've done about all I can do. I need to get someone out to look at the roof. But I'm just about through. Time to fix this place up now."

"I really wish you wouldn't sell, Cyl."

"Luna. Now's not the time to discuss that. Now's a time to enjoy each other."

"Fine. Then let's make out."

"Seriously?"

Luna answered Cyl with a powerful kiss that left her reeling. And needing more. Cyl kissed back with equal fervor and managed to get on top of Luna on the couch. She ground into Luna with her pelvis and Luna wrapped her legs around Cyl's hips and pulled them closer.

Cyl reached under Luna's blouse to caress her breast. She reached behind her and got her bra unhooked just as the doorbell rang.

"Shit," said Cyl.

"It's okay. I need to get home after dinner anyway. But, damn, that was fun"

"Yeah it was."

After dinner, Cyl walked Luna to her car and kissed her good night. It wasn't as passionate of a kiss because if it had been, Luna wouldn't have gone anywhere. And Cyl knew she needed to spend some time at her own place.

The next morning, Cyl was at the library when it opened. She scoured records for land titles for Cormac Byrne. She finally gave up and asked the librarian for help. Encouraged, she pulled up the Tax Collector Website and did a search.

She was about to give up when she found Cormac Byrne listed. It listed the coordinates of his property which didn't really help much. She'd need to find the grid that was used back then.

Back to the librarian who seemed eager to please. She pointed Cyl in the right direction yet again. Cyl found the old map of the city and checked out the coordinates. Damn. What the fuck? They were right where the lighthouse sat now.

Yes, they'd teased her about that, but she hadn't considered it a real possibility. So were Cormac and Aurnia buried on her property? The thought gave her the heebie-jeebies. She didn't like living next to dead people. Brigid being the obvious exception.

She sent a text to Luna.

Found out where their house was. I'm living there now.

There was no response so she figured Luna must be busy. She wanted to tell someone, anyone, but didn't want to disturb her friends. She drove home, stopped for a couple of six-packs, and popped the top off a cold one as soon as she was in the cottage.

Her phone rang and she was happy to hear from Luna. But it wasn't Luna. It was Martinique.

"Hello?" said Cyl.

"Luna forwarded me your text. Are you serious?"

"Dead. No pun intended."

"Very funny. Luna can't get away right now so she wanted me to check on you. How are you doing?"

"Not great. I suppose I'll walk out to the point tomorrow again and look for crosses or anything that might indicate they're buried here."

"Excellent idea. Cyl, this is really exciting."

"Is it though? Maybe we've gone far enough with this."

"Are you scared? Of what? Ghosts?"

"No. Not scared. More disgusted."

"Disgusted by what?" said Martinique.

"I don't know. Ghosts are fine. Actual dead bodies? I don't know about that."

"Yeah. I guess that would creep me out a bit, too."

"Thanks."

"Don't mention it. Well, I can clear my afternoon and come over if you need me."

"Thanks, Martinique. I do appreciate that. But I'll be okay. I'm just going to veg for a bit now."

"Okay. Well, I'm sure Luna will be over as soon as she can get away. Take care, Cyl."

"You, too."

Cyl opened another beer and took it to the gallery. It was cooler than usual up there and she figured Brigid must have been around. She didn't have the energy to strike up a conversation. The place warmed up and she knew Brigid was gone.

It was funny to think that her lighthouse was haunted. Like, a real, live ghost lived here. Who'd have thought that she'd not only cohabitate with a ghost, but that she'd believe it and be okay with it? She shook her head in disbelief. Tampa was changing her.

She was on her fourth beer when she heard tires on the driveway. She went downstairs to find Luna with an overnight bag. She grinned.

"I take it you're staying?" Cyl said.

"I don't really plan to, but I want to have options."

"Fair enough."

"How are you? Seriously?"

"Doin' better now." She held up her beer bottle. "I don't know. It's disconcerting to say the least."

"I'm sure it is. We don't know for sure they're buried here though, do we?"

"No. But where else would they be buried? The first cemetery in Tampa wasn't until the eighteen hundreds."

"Still. They could be buried in a church yard. That was common back then."

"That's true," said Cyl. "I hadn't considered that. We'll have to check that out. But not now. I want another beer. You want a glass of wine?"

"I'm taking you to dinner before you get any deeper into your beer collection. Come on."

Cyl was getting used to Ybor City. It was feeling familiar to her. Almost like home. But not. Because Tampa wasn't her home and never would be. So what was she doing with Luna? It didn't feel like a fling. God knows she'd had plenty of those. It felt right. She had no idea what she was doing.

They ate their burgers while Cyl sipped her Guinness and Luna nursed a glass of wine.

"You're awfully quiet. What's on your mind?" said Luna.

"Nothing, really. Just devouring dinner. I didn't realize I hadn't eaten all day. So thanks for making me get some grub."

"My pleasure. I'm a caregiver basically. I'll do my best not to mother you or smother you but know I'll always try to take care of you."

"Appreciate that."

"You're welcome."

Back at the cottage, Luna used Cyl's MacBook to search for churches with graveyards back in the sixteen hundreds. She wasn't finding much.

"What are you working on?" Cyl walked up behind her and nuzzled her neck.

"Looking for churches with graveyards."

"Any luck?"

"Not so far."

"So what if they're buried here?" Cyl said.

"That's the beer talking."

"Probably. Ugh. Dead bodies under my house don't appeal to me."

"I know, babe. But we don't know for sure they're here."

"We don't know they're not. Like I told Martinique, I'll go look for markers along the point tomorrow."

"I don't know if I want you to find them or not," Luna said.

"I think I do. So I'll know exactly where they are. I think I'd feel better."

"Well, I'm all about making you feel better. Which brings up a question I've been meaning to ask you."

"About feeling better? More beer. That's the answer."

"No. Before you get too fucked up to fuck. Do you have any toys?"

"Not with me. I didn't pack everything."

"That's what I was thinking." Luna winked. "I brought a few with me. Shall we try them out?"

"Sounds good to me."

Cyl's arousal was heightened by Luna's collection. She had a strap-on, some vibrators, and anal beads.

"You use those?" Cyl pointed to the beads.

"I have. But I have to really be in the right space for them."

"Gotcha. Let's get naked, Luna. You've got me all sorts of turned on."

"Sounds wonderful to me."

While making out like teenagers, they managed to get each other's clothes off. Naked, Cyl put on the strap-on and looked down at the dildo.

"You can really take all of this?"

"I don't know. It's brand new. I've never used any of these before. I bought them on the way over today."

"You vixen, you. I love it."

Cyl lay on her side on the bed, ready to devour Luna. Luna had other plans though, and Cyl watched Luna lick and suck her dildo. It was the fuckin hottest thing she'd ever seen. Luna took the length of it in her mouth and Cyl didn't know how she didn't gag. But she didn't.

"Get this inside of me, stud. I'm beyond ready for you."

Cyl positioned the cock at Luna's entrance and slid the tip in.

"More. I need more, Cyl."

"I don't want to hurt you." She slid it halfway in.

"Oh, dear God, that feels good. Ram the whole thing in. I can take it."

Cyl obliged. She shuddered at the feel of her thighs against Luna's, knowing her big cock was buried to its hilt. She moved it in and out over and over as Luna bucked off the bed taking each thrust.

Luna was barely coherent. She was making all kinds of noises but not much sense. Cyl was teetering on the edge herself. This was the hottest thing she'd ever experienced. Then Luna turned up the heat. She reached between her own legs and rubbed her clit and that's all it took for Cyl to sail into oblivion with the dildo buried inside Luna, who cried out at the same time.

"Holy shit," said Cyl when she could finally find her voice. "Holy. Fucking. Shit."

"That was pretty hot, huh?"

"That, my dear, is an understatement."

"I hope you didn't mind that I helped. I was just so close…"

"That was the icing on the cake, Luna. That's what sent me over the edge."

Cyl fell fast asleep but woke to a tugging on her hips in the middle of the night. Luna was sucking her cock again. Fully awake, Cyl moved to roll over for a repeat performance.

"Sh. You just roll onto your back. I'll take it from here," said Luna.

Cyl obeyed and watched as Luna straddled her and impaled herself on the waiting dildo.

"Oh shit," Cyl groaned. "Holy shit you're hot."

Cyl's thighs were soaked from Luna's juices, and she trembled with excitement as Luna neared her goal. She kept the dildo buried deep and was grinding into Cyl's pelvis. Luna cried Cyl's name and collapsed forward on top of her.

CHAPTER THIRTEEN

Luna was up and out of the house early to get to work. Cyl sipped her coffee and tried to find the motivation to go looking for grave markers. She wasn't feeling as gung ho about it as she had been under the influence of a few beers. She really didn't like the idea of dead people being so close to her. But she had to do it.

She walked out to the point as soon as the sun was up. She started there and zigzagged back toward the lighthouse. She had to stop and stretch periodically due to staring at the ground all the time. She was halfway back and was just about to give up. This seemed to be a futile venture.

At about fifty feet from the lighthouse, she found a crude cross. It was practically hidden by the grass, but she saw it. It seemed to be a grave marker. But there was only one. Where was the other one?

She doubled down her concentration in the area and found the other marker. The second cross had something carved in it, but it was hard to tell what it said. She didn't want to pick it up, but desperately wanted to know what was carved there.

Cyl went back to the cottage and got some soap and water. She carried the bucket out to the marker, sat down, and began scrubbing. Well, gently wiping anyway. She got most of the dirt off and could barely make out the carving, "Aurnia."

Wow. She'd found Aurnia's grave. And her cottage wasn't built on top of it. This made her feel significantly better. She snapped some pictures and sent them to Luna, Martinique, and Tawny. Then she headed back to the cottage, intent on getting some work done.

The outside shower left much to be desired. It was open for anyone to see you rinse off. She didn't like that. It made her uncomfortable. She jumped in the truck and went in search of lumber.

The shower was enclosed and had a bench when she finished up around six that evening. She checked her phone and found several missed texts. One from Martinique asking how she was feeling after finding the graves. And three from Luna checking in and then being worried that Cyl hadn't responded.

She shot Martinique a message saying she was fine and then sent Luna one saying she'd been working and hadn't had her phone on her. She apologized and asked if Luna would be over later.

Cyl was cleaning up her workspace when Luna pulled up.

"Do you not answer messages?" Luna was barely out of the car.

"I texted you back as soon as I saw them. Sorry. I was working. I was in my zone."

"Apology accepted. I was just worried sick knowing how you feel about dead bodies. And then I got in my head and started thinking you were avoiding me."

"Luna, you need to know one very important thing about me. I don't play games. If we had issues, I'd let you know. So, relax, come in, have some wine. It's all good."

"I'd like to see the graves," said Luna.

"Sure. Let's walk."

It was then Cyl decided to get some rocks to place around the graves so they'd be easier to find. Tomorrow. Chore numero uno.

She stopped and looked around.

"They're around here somewhere. They're not easy to see."

"We need to get proper markers then."

"I'll just get some rocks to mark the spots. I'll do that tomorrow."

"You don't think we should get gravestones?"

"I think that's a little extreme."

"Hm. Okay. It's your property."

"Tell you what," said Cyl. "We'll take a poll with the others. See what they think. Oh. Here we are."

She pointed to the cross with Aurnia's name on it.

"Wow. This is intense."

"Right?!"

"Yeah. Her spirit is restless but seems to be trapped. Very interesting."

"Restless? Trapped? How can a spirit be trapped? And how do you know these things?"

"I have a gift, remember?"

"Ah yes. One of many." Cyl winked.

"You're so irreverent."

Cyl shrugged.

"You ready for some wine now?"

"I suppose. I wish I'd thought to bring flowers."

"Next time, okay?"

"Yes. For sure."

Cyl opened a beer and poured Luna's wine. She found Luna in the master bedroom.

"What are you doing in here?"

"I'm curious. Have you emptied the desk?"

"Mostly. The two big drawers are filled with files I need to go through. Why?"

"I think Marjorie did a family tree. I'm just curious how far back she went."

"You thinking I'm related to Brigid? Or Aurnia?"

"It's possible." Luna took a sip of wine. "At this point, nothing would surprise me."

"I hear that. Hey, would you mind if I jumped in the shower? I am filthy from working all day."

"No problem. May I go through the drawers?"

Cyl wasn't sure she wanted Luna going through old tax returns and other financial data. Then she cautioned herself to calm down. If she was going to be with Luna, she had to trust her.

"Go for it."

"Thanks."

Cyl was out of the shower in less than ten minutes. She dried off then lay on the bed.

"Care to join me?"

"Oh, damn! There's an invitation I couldn't possibly pass up."

"Tease me," Cyl said. "Take off your clothes slowly."

Luna abided by her wishes and Cyl was throbbing by the time Luna was naked and lying beside her. She needed Luna in her and on her and more. But, ladies first. She kissed Luna hard on the mouth while she moved her hand to one voluptuous breast and then the other.

She kneaded the firm mounds before tugging on the nipples. Luna had the best breasts in the world. Bar none.

"You are so fucking sexy," Cyl said. "Words cannot describe what you do to me."

"Let me do you first then. If you think I'm so sexy. Can I go first?"

Cyl thought for a second. It kind of went against everything she believed in. But then, so did relationships and just look at her.

"If that would make you happy?"

"You have no idea," said Luna.

Cyl rolled onto her back and spread her legs. The AC felt amazing on her fevered flesh.

Luna sucked and nibbled Cyl's neck, causing gooseflesh. Cyl's nipples ached for attention.

Luna used her talented tongue like a pro on Cyl and she thought she would come from nipple play alone. That had never happened. And it didn't happen then either, but it had been close.

Luna kissed down Cyl's belly until she was between her legs.

"You are so fine," Luna said. "So fucking fine."

Without further ado, she bent her head and took Cyl in her mouth. Cyl lost the ability to think. All she could do was feel and dear God, what Luna made her feel. Luna had her tongue in her deep, then on her clit, then back inside. She felt amazing.

Cyl closed her eyes as her release drew near. Her whole body tensed.

"Oh, God, I'm going to come. Dear God, let me come."

And then she catapulted out of her body and into another realm where she stayed for a few seconds before floating back.

"Holy shit, that was intense," Cyl said.

"Yay for me."

"Oh indeed. Let me repay the favor now."

Cyl took Luna's wineglass from the nightstand and dribbled the wine over her tits, down her belly, and between her legs. Next, Cyl cleaned her up with her tongue. She licked and sucked Luna's breasts and nipples, then licked the wine trail off her soft stomach.

When she got to where Luna's legs met, Luna's own juices mixed with the wine and created a feast for Cyl.

"Yes," said Luna. "Yes. Yes. Yes!" She relaxed onto the bed, her grip on Cyl's head easing.

"Oh, my God," Luna spoke again. "I'm famished."

"I picked up a couple of steaks while I was out today. How does that sound?"

"Decadently delicious."

"Excellent. Let's get dressed and I'll fire up the grill."

Luna made the salad while Cyl grilled. They ate inside with Cyl complaining about the heat and humidity.

"I'm telling you, you get used to it," said Luna.

"And I'm telling you you're full of shit. No way anyone could get used to this swamp air."

Luna laughed.

"I'm not going to argue with you. But I'm also not complaining about eating in the air-conditioned cottage."

"Right?"

Luna did the dishes while Cyl started looking through the files in the desk. She found one that was labeled, "Family History." She hurried out to the dining room table.

"This looks promising," she said.

"Yes, it does. Open it. Let's see what we can see."

The tree started with Marjorie. Cyl's mom and dad were listed, as well as her grandparents. There was lots of information about them all. Cyl was shocked to see her parents' wedding announcement and her and her brother's birth announcements. Clearly, Aunt Marjorie had never given up on her family.

"I'm sure this is all really interesting to you, but can we fast-forward?" said Luna.

"Hm? Oh sure. Sorry. I did get distracted."

They flipped back to the eighteen hundreds and then back to the sixteen hundreds. They each took a sheet of paper and read over them. Cyl was lost in thought when Luna cried out.

"Oh, my God. I found it. Aurnia is an ancestor of yours!"

"Are you sure?" She leaned in to see what Luna was looking at.

"Aurnia Gallagher. It's right here. She was like your millionth aunt fifty times removed or something." They laughed. "But you're definitely related."

"Wow. Now I want to know who owned this property after the Byrnes."

"Good question. I wonder if it's been in your family since then."

"How cool would that be?"

"Way."

"No doubt," said Cyl. "No flippin' doubt."

Cyl wanted to be alone with this discovery. She needed to ponder it. But she couldn't very well ask Luna to leave.

"You're awfully quiet," said Luna.

"Just taking it all in. It's a lot of information. I need to be alone for a while. Would you mind if I took a beer up to the gallery for a bit?"

"Not at all. I can leave if you like."

"Thank you. But I couldn't ask you to. Besides, you've had too much wine to drive now. I'll just go absorb it up there."

"Okay. I'm going to keep studying. I want to see if I can figure out who has owned the lighthouse and when."

"Good luck with that."

"Thanks."

Cyl took a sip of beer as she stared out across the dark gulf. Aurnia was her relative. Aurnia was a lesbian? She was Brigid's lover, so she had to be. But she was married. Hell, what did that mean? She'd known plenty of lesbians who'd come out later in life.

So Aurnia was a lesbian. And Aunt Marjorie was a lesbian. And now Cyl was a lesbian. Coincidence? Cyl didn't think so. She wasn't a true believer in coincidences. Was it possible the place had been left to lesbians this whole time? She was determined to find out.

She hurried down the stairs and found Luna poring over the family tree.

"Look for single women," said Cyl.

"What? Why?"

"I think this place has been handed down to lesbians over the years."

"That sounds pretty far-fetched."

"I don't know. Aurnia? Aunt Marjorie? Me? Come on, Luna. Think about it."

"You may be on to something. But Aurnia wasn't single."

"True." Cyl sat down and exhaled. "So maybe all the owners of this property were lesbians, but not necessarily out and proud."

"You could be right. I mean, why else would Marjorie have left it to you?"

"Right? Who did Marjorie get it from?"

"That's a question for another day. It's getting late and I'm getting tired. Do you mind if I turn in?"

"Go for it. I'll just spend a little more time with this family tree and I'll be right in."

Chapter Fourteen

Cyl was at the rock shop when it opened the next morning. She surveyed all the stones that were offered, but couldn't find just the right ones. Then she found a section of river-washed stones and chose twelve of the biggest ones they had.

It took her a minute to find the graves again, but when she did, she placed a circle of rocks around each. She wished she'd thought to pick up some flowers but seemed to remember Luna saying she would bring some.

She stood staring at the graves and wondered if she should have bought more stones and made a circle for Brigid on the other side of Aurnia. It seemed like it would be fitting. And maybe Brigid would rest if she did that.

Back at the shop, Cyl bought six more stones and placed them in a circle just as she'd planned. She walked out to the point looking for pieces of wood or even just some sticks to make a cross. She found some old pieces of wood and took them back to the lighthouse.

Cyl burned Brigid's name into the wood and made a makeshift cross. She went back down the property and placed the cross at the head of the circle. Not that Cyl knew which end was up, but she put it where she imagined Brigid's head would be if she could ever lay and rest.

It was time to put some serious work into the cottage. She'd been there over six weeks and leaving was nowhere in sight. She needed to get busy.

But she wasn't feeling it. What she wanted to do was look over the family tree again. The cottage could wait one more day. She made a sandwich and settled in to do more research.

So she knew Marjorie had left the lighthouse to her. Her first order of business was to figure out who'd left it to Marjorie. That would hopefully be in another folder in the desk.

Cyl went back to her bedroom and sat at the desk. She pulled out both the big drawers, stuffed with paper, and wondered where to look first. She opted for the drawer on the left since that was where she'd found the family tree.

There were receipts from tree trimmers to grocery deliveries. Ugh. So much wasted paper. Cyl was astounded that her aunt hadn't been more ecoconscious. But then, she was older so maybe it made sense.

She pulled out four folders and placed them on her desk. She went through the first two and knew she'd have to come back to them. Papers that were obviously important to Aunt Marjorie, but they weren't what Cyl was looking for.

In the third folder, she found the deed to the property. Included was the last will and testament of a Kerry Walsh in which the property was left to Marjorie O'Connor. Kerry Walsh? The name didn't sound familiar.

She went back out to the dining room and placed the will next to the pile of papers that was the family tree. She searched for the original page with Aunt Marjorie on it. She followed the line up two generations to a Kerry Walsh. Sure enough, they were related. Kerry didn't have a husband attached to her. Curiouser and curiouser.

Kerry had lived from eighteen ninety-five to nineteen seventy. And she'd never been married. Cyl searched the accompanying paperwork and found Kerry's obituary. She was survived by her longtime friend, Sarah McIlroy. So why hadn't she left the lighthouse to Sarah? Because it had to stay in the family. But why?

So who had left the lighthouse to Kerry? This could prove trickier. She'd need to search titles going back over a hundred years. But she needed to know. She pulled up the title search site and entered her address.

The owner before Kerry Walsh was one Ciara Murphy. Hence the Old Murphy Lighthouse. Back to the family tree. Sure enough. There was Ciara Murphy. Damn. So the lighthouse had been in the family since it was built.

Ciara had owned and operated a saloon in town before providing much of the funding for the lighthouse. She had lived in the cottage on the property before the lighthouse was built, but then agreed that it was needed so offered the majority of the money needed to build it.

Her saloon must have done very well. The other thing Cyl noticed was that these women lived to ripe old ages. Except Aunt Marjorie. Her life was cut short. That was very sad.

She was about to resume her title search when she heard a knock on the door. It was Luna. It was already five thirty? The day had flown by.

Cyl opened the door with a smile and pulled Luna to her.

"You're going to crush these flowers," said Luna.

"Aurnia won't care." Cyl laughed. "I've had the most interesting day and can't wait to tell you about it."

"I'm all ears. Tell me as we walk to Aurnia's grave."

"Sounds good."

Cyl proceeded to tell Luna everything she had learned that day as they walked out to the circles of rocks.

"That's awesome. I had a feeling that's what we would find. Wait. Why are there three circles?"

"One's for Brigid. If she decides she wants to rest."

"Very thoughtful."

"Thank you."

Luna set the flowers on Aurnia's grave, and they stood in silence, each lost in their own thoughts. Cyl was pondering what an amazing woman Aurnia must have been and wondered how she ended up nursing Brigid back to health. How had they met? Cyl was determined to find out.

It wasn't like they had medical ships back then. And how had Aurnia happened to be at the exact spot to help Brigid? So many questions. Too many. Only Brigid would be able to answer them.

"We've got to talk to Brigid," she said.

"We will. It's almost time."

"I don't know if I can wait until Friday."

"You'll have to. Make a list of questions now. While you're thinking of them."

Cyl did just that. She opened the Notes section of her phone and typed out questions for Brigid. She didn't know how many Brigid would be able to answer, but at least she had a game plan now.

"I've got to say, you're way more into this than I thought you'd be. I'm actually impressed."

Cyl shrugged.

"What can I say? I've got a curious nature."

"That you have. And now, I'm famished. I want a huge chef salad for dinner. Come on. My treat."

Cyl's stomach growled. She'd only had a sandwich that day and her stomach was clearly unhappy with that.

"Sure. I could go for a nice salad myself."

"You're in for a treat."

Luna drove to a restaurant in where else? Ybor City.

"Do you work here, too?" said Cyl.

"I wish. My studio is downtown."

They had just sat down when Martinique walked up.

"Fancy meeting you two here."

"Martinique! So good to see you," said Luna. "Can you join us?"

"I wish. Long day. I'm heading home. But I'm curious if y'all have learned anything new?"

"Cyl found Cormac's and Aurnia's graves."

"That's exciting."

"It is," said Cyl. "And I've done some research on the history of the property. Seems like it's been in the family since Aurnia lived there."

"Really? So you're related to Aurnia?"

"I am indeed."

Martinique rubbed her arms.

"Goose bumps," she said.

"Will you be over Friday night?" said Luna.

"I will indeed. I think Tawny is going to try to join us as well."

"Excellent," said Cyl. "We'll have the whole gang back together."

"Yes, we will. Now, I'll leave you two to your dinner. I've got to go home and collapse. I'll see y'all in a couple of days."

Back at the cottage after dinner, Cyl sat down in front of her computer again. Luna stood behind her and rubbed her shoulders.

"You're so tense," Luna said.

"Mm."

"You need to relax."

"I'm sorry. I'm just so fascinated by all this."

"Well, step away from it all. Let's have a relaxing evening. I'll pour myself a glass of wine and you should have a beer."

Cyl closed her MacBook.

"You're right. Thanks. What shall we do to relax?"

"Let's snuggle on the couch."

"I'll meet you there."

Snuggling led to kissing which led to making out which led to hands roaming all over each other, on top of and under clothes. Cyl was so aroused she thought she might climax just from the teasing.

"I've got to have you," she whispered.

"Take me."

Cyl pulled Luna's slacks and underwear down and closed her mouth on the paradise she found. She savored every drop and moved her tongue over every swollen inch. Luna tasted divine and Cyl couldn't get enough.

She used her fingers inside Luna then and focused all her attention on Luna's clit. She sucked and licked and finally Luna let out a guttural moan and relaxed. Cyl moved up and kissed her hard on her mouth.

"That's the most fun I've ever had with my clothes on, I think," said Luna.

"Sorry. I got a little frantic."

"Now it's my turn to return the favor." Luna unzipped Cyl's shorts. She slid her hand in and Cyl groaned as Luna's fingers found her center. She thrust them so deep and Cyl needed more. She wanted her deeper, harder.

Luna rubbed all the special spots inside Cyl before dragging her fingers to Cyl's clit. Her clit was aching she needed release so desperately. It didn't take long before Cyl cried out Luna's name and soared high above herself.

"Now," said Luna. "Can we go to bed and make love like normal people?"

"Define normal." Cyl laughed.

They got naked and Cyl put on the strap-on.

"I need you carnally. I could make love to you tenderly, but that's not what I'm in the mood for."

"You want to fuck me. Just say it."

"I want to fuck your brains out."

Luna got on all four and wagged her ass.

"Fuck me, Cyl. I want to feel the end of that dildo in my mouth."

"Oh, shit. Now you're talking."

Cyl thrust her hips and filled Luna in one motion. Luna's juices flowed over the hilt and ran down Cyl's thighs. It was so fucking hot. Cyl had never, ever been more turned on.

She continued to fuck Luna until Luna screamed and collapsed face first into the pillow.

"My turn," Luna said.

Cyl lay back and spread her legs.

"Do me then."

"Not so fast." Luna removed the dildo from its harness. She looked from the dildo to Cyl's pussy and back again. "Let's see what you can take."

"What?"

Luna slid the dildo halfway into Cyl.

"More," Cyl growled.

Luna buried the toy inside Cyl and Cyl moved all around, taking it as deep as she could. She started panting as she grew nearer and nearer to nirvana. Then Luna stopped.

"What the—" Cyl wasn't ready to stop, but she didn't complain as she watched Luna fucking herself with the silicone cock. It was too hot to watch. Cyl started frantically rubbing her clit as she watched Luna's eyes glaze over and knew she was going to come again.

Luna cried out and Cyl followed close behind.

"Damn, you're hot," said Cyl. "I know I've told you before, but I mean it. You are so fucking hot!"

"I'm glad you think so. Sorry to have interrupted you, but the sight of you swallowing this got me super horny again. I had to have another orgasm.

"Far be it from me to deprive you an orgasm."

"I appreciate that."

They snuggled together again and soon Cyl heard Luna's breathing even out. She knew she was asleep, but, although satiated, Cyl still couldn't sleep. Her mind continued to race with thoughts about the history of the lighthouse and the women who had owned it before her.

Chapter Fifteen

Friday night finally arrived. The four of them sat around the table in the entry to the lighthouse. Cyl turned off the lights and the temperature immediately dropped. Brigid was obviously ready for them.

She tapped on the table and Luna greeted her.

"Good evening, Brigid. Thanks for meeting with us."

"Do you spend your days looking for Aurnia?" said Cyl. One knock.

"Cyl found her," said Martinique.

"She's buried not far from here. Would you like us to show you?" One knock.

"Great. This way," Luna said.

Cyl led the way with a flashlight.

"How do we know Brigid's still with us?" Tawny said.

"Why wouldn't she be?" said Luna.

Cyl stopped and shined the light on Aurnia's cross. She watched as the flowers Luna had brought were moved as if of their own accord.

"I set up this area for you." Cyl pointed to the third circle. "In case you want to settle down someday."

The flowers crashed to the ground. What the hell did that mean? Was that a hard no?

"Let's get back to the lighthouse," said Luna.

Once inside, they held hands around the table again.

"Brigid? Are you here?" Luna said. One knock.

"You okay?" said Cyl. One knock.

"When you crashed," said Tawny, "was there a treasure on your ship?" One knock.

The other three looked at Tawny in disbelief. She hadn't said a word all night and now she was only interested in the treasure?

"Was it ever recovered?" Two knocks. "Interesting."

"Was Aurnia married when you met her?" Luna seemed intent on getting back to the love story. Brigid knocked hard on the table.

"We're you lovers?" said Cyl. "Or we're you simply in love with her?"

"That's two questions," said Martinique.

"Sorry. Were you lovers?" One knock.

"Ah," Luna said. "Star-crossed lovers." A soft knock

"Was her husband alive when you met?" Martinique spoke up. One knock.

"Was her husband traveling with her when you met?" said Cyl. One knock. "Did their ship try to save yours?" Another knock.

"How long did you know Aurnia?" said Luna.

The pen hovered over the paper then.

A fortnight.

"And then what happened?" asked Martinique.

I died.

The group sat in stunned silence. How sad. To meet who you're sure is the love of your life and only know them for two weeks. It sounded unbearable, even to Cyl.

"So you came here and have been waiting for her ever since?" said Luna. One knock.

"Did she come back here? After you died?" Cyl said.

No.

"No? Then whose graves are those out there?"

Don't know.

The pen fell to the table.

"Are you getting tired, Brigid?" said Luna. One knock.

"Okay," said Cyl. "We'll let you go. Would you like to visit again tomorrow night?" One knock.

"Okay then," said Luna. "We'll see you then."

Cyl waited a beat but soon the room warmed up so she turned on the lights.

"Damn," said Martinique. "What a sad tale."

"No doubt," Cyl said.

They walked back to the cottage where Cyl poured drinks.

"You were awfully quiet, Tawny," said Martinique.

"Just taking it all in."

"Yeah," Cyl said. "There was a lot to take in."

"Thanks for the drink," Tawny said. "But I'm going to hit it. I need to be at work tomorrow. I'll be back tomorrow night."

"Great. We'll see you then," said Luna.

Luna, Martinique, and Cyl sat sipping their drinks in silence.

"What did you think about the treasure?" Cyl said. "Do you suppose it's still out there?"

"If it is, it's at the bottom of a deep body of water," said Luna. "No one is going to get it now."

"That's probably true," Martinique said.

"We could charter a boat and go look for it."

"How? We wouldn't even know where to start. I say we start with figuring out where Aurnia died," said Luna.

"I think you're right," said Martinique. "But not tonight. I need to get some sleep. You two enjoy your night and I'll see you tomorrow night."

"You want to meet us at the library tomorrow?" said Cyl. "We could make a day of it."

"Maybe. Text me, okay?"

"You got it."

Alone with Luna, Cyl's thoughts turned to more enjoyable things than Aurnia's death. But Luna was already focused on the MacBook.

"Find anything?" Cyl said.

"Not yet. It's gotta be out there somewhere though. Somewhere there's a record of Aurnia's death. I just don't know how to search."

"I'm telling you. The library will have a record of it."

"Yeah, but I want to find it now." Luna laughed.

"And I want you now."

"Mm. That sounds more fun than staring at this screen."

"I thought so."

Cyl took her time with Luna. They made out fully dressed until Luna was writhing on the bed, grinding against Cyl. Cyl finally took mercy on her.

"Shall we get undressed?" she said.

"Dear God, please."

They lay skin to skin and Cyl struggled with the sensations. Luna was so soft and silky, and she turned Cyl on like she'd never been turned on before. She forced herself to go slowly, to not rush, to draw out the pleasure. It wasn't easy.

Cyl nibbled down Luna's neck and got comfortable on her ample bosom. She sucked and licked the luscious mounds before closing her mouth around a hard nipple and sucking it deep.

Luna moaned her appreciation and Cyl kept on doing what she was doing. She loved how responsive Luna was. She realized Luna was moving her arm and opened her eyes to see Luna stroking herself.

"What are you doing?" said Cyl.

"Feeling good."

"Let me join you."

"Will you touch yourself for me, Cyl? Please?"

Cyl rolled off and slid her hand between her own legs. She watched as Luna's clit swelled and listened to the sounds of Luna pleasing herself. The combo was too much and Cyl rubbed her own clit until she rocketed into orbit. It was a powerful, muscle tensing orgasm. She hadn't expected that due to the fact she hardly ever took matters into her own hands. But Luna was so fucking arousing that it would have been hard not to come.

They slept late the following morning so stopped for breakfast on their way to the library Cyl had texted Martinique but hadn't heard back. No biggie. She and Luna could handle the task at hand.

Over coffee while waiting for their food, Luna smiled at Cyl.

"What are you thinking?" said Cyl.

"Last night was hot," Luna said.

"It was. I was surprised at how hot it was."

"You're sexy as hell when you come," said Luna.

"As are you."

"Thank you."

They finished their breakfast and headed to the library. Luna surprised Cyl by taking her hand when they got out of Mabel. She wasn't usually the public display of affection type, but there was no harm, Cyl figured.

They found the old death records of Hillsborough County. The first few volumes only covered the nineteenth and twentieth centuries. They pulled four more volumes and split them up to look for any information on Aurnia.

"Got it," Cyl said.

"What?"

"Aurnia died on a ship in the Caribbean. She died of consumption. Poor thing."

"I wonder if she died right after Brigid. Maybe she really died of a broken heart?"

Cyl smiled at Luna.

"You're such a romantic."

"Guilty as charged."

"Apparently, Aurnia was buried at sea. So the cross in my yard is just a place marker. It doesn't mark an actual grave."

"I wish we could bring Aurnia home."

"So do I, babe. But I don't see that happening."

"No. I don't suppose it's feasible."

"Not at all," said Cyl.

Cyl shot Martinique a text to let her know they were leaving.

"Can we look at the old maps of the Caribbean?" said Luna. "Just to look?"

"There's no harm in looking, but don't get your hopes up."

They got to the old maps section to find Tawny poring over a map at one of the tables.

"What are you doing here?" said Luna. "I thought you had to work today."

"I work in an hour." Tawny looked perturbed at the interruption.

"What are you doing looking at these maps?"

"Trying to get a feel for Brigid. Wondering where she died."

"We just found out Aurnia died in the Caribbean as well," said Cyl.

"Really? That's too bad."

"It really is."

"Well, I should go get ready for work. I'll see y'all tonight."

"Bye, Tawny," said Cyl.

"She didn't seem too happy to see us," said Luna.

"No. She seemed pissed. I wonder what's going on with her."

"We can ask her tonight. Let's check out these maps now."

All the maps did was reinforce that the chances of finding Aurnia were slim to none. The Caribbean may not have been the biggest sea, but it was big enough that there was virtually no way to figure out where Aurnia might be.

"Wait," said Luna. "If we could find what ship she was on, we could track the route it was on. Then we could pinpoint where Aurnia died."

"That's a good point," said Cyl. "Really good idea. We could also look up the *Tainted Rose*. We still don't know where Brigid's ship went down. If we can find that out, we'd be able to narrow down where Aurnia died."

"Cyl. You're a genius. Let's start scouring old ship records."

"Where though? Like, where would we even start?"

"I don't know."

"You wait here. I'll go ask the librarian where the books on ships and their travels would be."

Cyl was back a few minutes later.

"Come on," she said. "It's across the library."

They found volumes upon volumes on ships and their voyages.

"Where to start?" said Luna.

"It looks like they're listed alphabetically by ship. Let's look for the Ts."

They found seven volumes on ships that started with T. Undaunted, they took the first three and searched for *Tainted Rose*.

"Got it," said Luna. "I found *Tainted Rose*. Let's check it out. We can look over it at home. I've about spent enough time in the library for one day."

They got home and Luna studied the information on *Tainted Rose* while Cyl put together dinner. They ate and sat together while Luna continued to read about Brigid's ship.

"Nothing yet?" said Cyl.

"It's fascinating. She was quite a pirate. I could just flip to the end, but I've been caught up in reading of her adventures."

"Why am I not surprised?" Cyl laughed.

"She was a complete badass. She had an almost all female crew and they were hell on the high seas."

"That's awesome."

"It really is."

A knock on the door reminded them how late it was. Martinique was there with wine and beer.

"Come in," said Cyl. "And thank you."

"Did we learn anything today?"

"Only that Brigid was a goddess among pirates," said Luna.

"Why am I not surprised?" Martinique said.

"We also learned that Aurnia died of consumption. We're trying to figure out if it was right after she tried to save Brigid or not. Right now we're trying to get to the end of Brigid's reign, but Luna is too busy reading about her life to fast-forward to her death."

"I can understand that. So did we learn where Aurnia died?"

"On a ship in the Caribbean," said Cyl. "Hence the curiosity of where Brigid's ship went down."

"Now I see the connection. Interesting," said Martinique. "Now why don't you pour the wine?"

"Ah. Excellent idea."

Cyl gave them their drinks and sat and watched as Martinique looked over Luna's shoulder.

"She was amazing," said Martinique. "Just this little bit I'm reading? No wonder Luna has been fascinated."

"Right?" Luna said.

"Well, I think you should close the book and finish your wine. Tawny should be here any minute. And I'd hate to keep Brigid the badass waiting."

CHAPTER SIXTEEN

It was ten thirty and there was still no sign of Tawny. Martinique texted her to see where she was.

Not gonna make it tonight.

"That's weird," said Martinique. "No explanation or anything. Very unlike Tawny."

"She was at the library studying the Caribbean when we were there today," said Cyl. "She seemed excited about tonight."

"Yeah she did. Oh well. Let's go see Brigid."

They summoned Brigid for forty-five minutes. Cyl was just about to call it quits when they felt the temperature cool and heard a knock.

"Are you okay tonight?" said Luna. One soft knock.

"Did last night take it out of you?" said Cyl. Another knock.

"Do you want to take tonight off?" Luna said. Two knocks.

"We went to the library today," said Cyl. "We took out a book about *Tainted Rose*. And learned about Aurnia's death. Did she die shortly after she met you?" One knock.

"Did it upset you that they didn't bring her back here to be buried properly?" said Luna. One knock.

"And you've hung around here this whole time waiting for her to come home?" Martinique said. One knock.

"Damn," Cyl said softly. She was getting more determined by the minute to find Aurnia and bring her home to rest.

"We learned a lot about you today," said Luna. "You had quite an impressive life."

"Do you miss being a pirate?" Martinique said. One knock. "I bet."

"You spent most of your time in the Caribbean," said Luna. "Is that where you were from?" Two knocks.

The pen hovered over the paper. It wavered slightly and Cyl wondered if they'd taken up too much of Brigid's time.

Ireland.

"Damn," Cyl said again. "So you sailed all the way from there to the Caribbean?" One knock.

"Impressive," said Martinique. "Were you a pirate the whole way?" Two knocks.

"Yeah," said Luna. "Because there was no mention of the *Tainted Rose* in the Atlantic." Two knocks.

"So you sailed from Ireland to the Caribbean and then decided to be a pirate?" Martinique said. One knock.

"Cool," said Cyl. "What made you decide to be a pirate?"

The pen hovered again.

Fun.

Cyl laughed.

"I could see that."

They sat in silence for a few moments before Brigid picked up the pen again.

Tired.

"Okay," said Luna. "That's enough for one night."

They said their thank yous and promised to be back soon. The room grew warm and Cyl turned on the lights.

"Damn," she said. "I wish we could have proper conversations with her. There is so much I'd like to ask her."

"I agree," said Martinique. "I'd love to just chat with her."

"She's fascinating. No doubt," Luna said.

"I need something stronger than wine," Martinique said as they entered the cottage. "How about a rum and Coke?"

"Rum? How appropriate," said Cyl. "Coming right up."

"By the way, I'm spending the night tonight. Just letting you know. I'm going to get tipsy."

"Fair enough," said Luna. "There's always the spare room."

"Thank you."

"Any particular reason we're getting tipsy?" Cyl said.

"I don't know. Frustration at not being able to properly converse with Brigid. Annoyance that she and Aurnia aren't together in the afterworld. Who knows? I just feel like it."

"Well, no judgment. And I think that's a great idea. I'll have some bourbon."

"I wish I liked the hard stuff," said Luna. "I'll stick to wine. I'll be the head of reason I suppose."

They all laughed and settled in at the dining room table.

"Let me read about the *Tainted Rose*," said Martinique.

Luna pushed the book toward her.

"I've bookmarked where it starts and haven't got to the end yet."

"Right."

Cyl and Luna watched Martinique read. Cyl finished her drink and got up to make another one. She may as well get shitfaced since she and Luna obviously weren't about to have sex with Martinique in the house.

"Where did she spend most of her time?" Cyl said.

"Grand Cayman Island," said Luna. "She seemed to use that as her headquarters and sailed to other islands to attack ships."

"Fast-forward," said Cyl. "Let's skip to the end. Y'all can go back and read the other stuff later. Let's see what happened when she died."

"Fine. But it'll cost you another drink."

"Coming right up."

Cyl mixed another rum and Coke and brought it to the table. Luna and Martinique had their heads pressed together reading. Damn, they looked hot together. Cyl told herself to calm down. She wasn't having a three-way with those two. That could be deadly.

"Apparently, she ran into rocks off the coast of Hispaniola," said Martinique.

"Yeah. That's what it says," said Luna. "So now we know where she died. We just need to figure out how to place Aurnia there and then figure out where she was when she died."

Cyl opened up her MacBook and googled Hispaniola to get a feel of the coastline. She had to see it. Had to feel it. She felt such a connection with Brigid and Aurnia. Brigid more so, even though she was related to Aurnia.

"What are you looking at?" Martinique was standing behind her rubbing her shoulders.

"Just trying to get a feel for Hispaniola. I don't know. Somehow I want to know everything there is to know about Brigid and Aurnia."

"I think we all do," said Martinique.

The clock chimed two o'clock. Luna shut the book.

"I think it's time for bed. What do you say?"

"Will you two be having sex while I'm here?" said Martinique.

"We'll be more respectful than that," said Cyl.

"Why don't we all have sex together?" said Luna. "I've always been curious about you, Martinique. No pressure, though."

Before Cyl could protest, Martinique nibbled her neck.

"That sounds wonderful."

"I don't want to do anything to make things awkward between the three of us," Cyl said.

"No awkwardness. Scout's honor," said Martinique.

Shit. Cyl wasn't about to kick two beautiful ladies out of her bed. Martinique continued to nibble Cyl's neck while she moved her hands to fondle Cyl's breasts.

"Hey now," said Luna. "Don't forget me."

She got up and spun Martinique around and kissed her, hard on the mouth. Cyl stood on shaky legs and watched the hot scene unfold. Hands were roaming over each other and Cyl wanted her hands and mouth on both of them. And she didn't want to wait another minute.

"Let's take this to the bedroom," she said.

"Don't rush things." Martinique stepped away from Luna and kissed Cyl full on the mouth. She ran her hand between Cyl's legs, pulled back and smiled. "Someone is ready."

"Beyond."

While Martinique kissed Cyl, Luna unzipped Martinique's skirt and watched it fall to the floor. She squatted down and took

Martinique's thong off with her teeth. Martinique's trimmed pussy on display was almost too much for Cyl to handle.

She reached to stroke it, but Martinique stepped away.

"You're in such a hurry," she said. "Slow down. Enjoy the process."

Martinique turned to Luna, showing her tight ass to Cyl, who cupped it and grew dizzy with need. Martinique took Luna's top off and unhooked her bra, freeing her full breasts.

"Damn," Martinique said. She lowered her head and sucked one nipple then the other.

Cyl took her shirt off and was about to step out of her shorts.

"Slow down, Turbo," said Martinique. "It'll be your turn in a minute."

"I don't have a minute. I need both of you now."

Martinique lowered Cyl's shorts and boxers and dragged her hand over Cyl's wetness.

"Yum," she said. She licked her fingers clean, touched herself, then placed her fingers in Luna's mouth.

"Delicious," said Luna.

"Let's get you out of those shorts." Martinique lowered Luna's shorts then bent and took her panties off with her teeth, returning the favor. She dragged her tongue along Luna, who held onto Cyl's shoulders to maintain her balance. Martinique stood and kissed Cyl hard on the mouth, sharing Luna's flavor with her.

Cyl's brain was foggy with lust. She was hyperaware of the two nude beauties in front of her and didn't know how much longer she could be patient.

"Lie on the couch, Cyl," said Martinique. "I want to look at your pussy."

"You could see it just as well in bed," said Cyl.

"Are we doing this or not?" said Martinique.

Cyl lay on the couch.

"One leg on the floor and one leg over the back of the couch."

Cyl felt awkward but did as Martinique instructed. Anything to get fucked at that point.

"You're gorgeous," said Martinique.

"Isn't she?" said Luna.

"Touch yourself for me, Cyl."

Cyl dragged her hand between her legs, careful to avoid her clit which was close to exploding. Martinique lowered herself onto the couch and took Cyl in her mouth while Luna knelt next to the couch and sucked on Cyl's nipples.

Cyl's head was spinning. Luna and Martinique had her feeling things she hadn't felt in a long while. Yes, Luna turned her on, but this took it to the next level. Martinique's tongue was probing, demanding, and Cyl pressed Martinique's face into her pussy, holding her in place while she silently begged for release.

Martinique's tongue continued to work its magic while Luna expertly licked and sucked her tits. Cyl couldn't hold on much longer. She felt the white heat coil in her center. Her whole body tensed. One more flick of Martinique's tongue and the coil released, shooting the heat throughout her extremities.

"Holy fuck!" Cyl cried out as she came.

"That was fun," said Luna.

"Indeed," said Cyl. "But now it's time to treat the ladies. Bed. Now."

They fell onto the bed, Martinique and Luna in a passionate embrace. They were lost in their kisses and Cyl got comfortable below them on the bed. She plunged her fingers into Luna while her mouth sought Martinique's center. She was delicious with a musky flavor that Cyl savored once again.

She added another finger and then another to Luna until Luna gasped and seemed to forget Martinique was there. She rolled onto her back and tweaked her nipples while Cyl continued to fuck her with her fingers.

Martinique's breath was coming in short gasps and Cyl knew she was close. She continued to suck Martinique's clit until both Martinique and Luna screamed and reached their orgasms at the same time.

Cyl was horny again but didn't know how much the other two had left. She had to be aware of their needs as well.

"Do you have any toys?" said Martinique.

"A few. Not many. Luna bought some recently."

"Where are they?"

"In my top dresser drawer."

Martinique returned with the dildo and a vibrator.

"Lie back, Cyl," she said.

She handed the dildo to Luna.

"Have fun," she said. Martinique turned on the vibrator and ran it along Cyl's cheek and down her neck.

"Do you want this on your clit?" Martinique said.

"Yes."

"Not so fast."

Cyl was full from the dildo that Luna kept shoving deep and pressing against her before pulling it back out and thrusting it again.

Martinique placed the vibrator against Cyl's nipple and Cyl cried out forgetting to try and hold off. She came fast and furious. And wasn't ashamed.

"We should get some sleep now," said Martinique.

"What about you two?" said Cyl.

"I'm fine for now. I prefer morning sex anyway."

"Luna?"

"Take me again, Cyl."

Cyl donned her strap-on and Luna got on all fours to take it in. When she knew Luna was close, Cyl reached around and rubbed her clit until Luna cried out and collapsed on top of Martinique.

"Sweet dreams," said Martinique.

"No doubt," said Cyl.

"See you in the morning," Luna murmured as she drifted off to dreamland.

CHAPTER SEVENTEEN

Cyl woke to an empty bed. What happened to morning sex? She looked at the clock. It was nine thirty. Dang. She never slept that late. She didn't bother to put any clothes on and wandered out to find Martinique and Luna sitting at the dining room table reading the book again.

"You two feel like coming back to bed?" Cyl said.

"Damn. Look at you," said Martinique. "I'm on my way."

Luna followed and they all pleased each other until no one had anything left.

"Nap time?" said Martinique.

"I say it's food time. And then library," said Luna.

"I'm starving," said Cyl.

"Fine. I'm getting up."

They took Mabel into town and had breakfast at the first diner Cyl had stopped at when she'd gotten Mabel.

"This is where we met," said Luna.

"Indeed it is."

The three were greeted like old friends by the hostess. They were seated and quickly decided what they'd have. Then talk turned to Brigid and Aurnia.

"I'm thinking if the *Tainted Rose* sunk near the shore, the treasure has already been found," said Cyl.

"You'd think Brigid would know that," said Martinique.

"Yes. I agree. I think the ship is still out there somewhere."

"Okay. So now we need to put Aurnia at the same place. How can we determine that?"

"Maybe she was in Hispaniola on holiday," said Martinique. "That's the only thing I can think of that would explain it."

"Yeah. That's what I'm thinking too," said Cyl.

"But we need to find out for sure. We need to find a passenger list for a ship that sailed there during that time. How are we going to do that?" said Luna.

"I'm sure Brigid would know the name of Aurnia's ship. But we haven't asked her and don't get to talk to her for another week." Cyl didn't try to hide her frustration.

"Why don't we ask her tonight?" said Martinique. "Is there a rule that we can't try to summon her on a Sunday night?"

"But you two have to work tomorrow," said Cyl.

"Well, I won't spend the night again, unfortunately," Martinique said.

"I don't mind staying up. I'd like to ask Brigid," said Luna.

"Okay. Then that's settled. So what's the point of going to the library then?"

"Good point. Oh good. Our food's here," said Martinique.

They ate and Cyl paid, over Martinique's objections.

"I'm buying dinner," she said.

"Is that right?" said Cyl.

"Yes. We'll spend the day together and then I'll take us out to dinner."

"Sounds good to me," said Luna. "What shall we do with our day?"

"Let's go to St. Pete," said Cyl. "I could use some fun in the sun."

They all met back at the cottage an hour later with Martinique and Luna looking stunning in their suits with towels wrapped around their waists. Cyl wanted to take them both back to bed. Was she being untrue to Luna? It didn't seem that way since Luna was a willing participant.

"You both look good enough to eat," said Cyl.

"Later, stud," said Luna.

"Color me jealous," said Martinique.

"You're invited," Luna said.

"I just might take you up on that."

"I hope you will."

The sun and the water were just what Cyl needed. The three of them played and swam, then lay on their towels and soaked up rays. Cyl dozed and woke up alone for the second time that day. She propped herself up on her elbows and saw Luna and Martinique bobbing in the waves.

She joined them and they moved deeper where the water was up to Luna's shoulders.

"I can't go any deeper," said Luna.

"I can," said Cyl. She moved Luna's crotch to the side and entered her.

"You're so nasty," said Luna. "I love it."

"You've got two hands," said Martinique. "Let's see if you're ambidextrous."

Cyl gave it her best shot. She felt clumsy with her left hand but managed to move around inside both women at once. Then she found their clits and Luna and Martinique buried their faces in Cyl's shoulders as they cried out.

Feeling insanely proud of herself, Cyl walked back to the shore. She needed to lie down again. She barely trusted her legs. Martinique and Luna followed her and stood over her dripping wet.

"You're dripping on me," said Cyl.

"You weren't complaining a minute ago," said Martinique.

They lay down and they snoozed for a half hour. Martinique woke them up.

"I need a shower and dinner. Who's with me?"

"Sounds divine," said Luna.

"Let's go then," said Cyl.

The shower at the house was barely big enough for two.

"You two shower together. I'll use the outside shower. I'll be in in a minute."

"I can't promise to keep my hands off your girlfriend," said Martinique.

"I can't blame you. You two have fun."

Cyl's imagination ran wild as she got the salt and sand off her. She could only imagine the fun the others were having. She wasn't jealous, per se. She was sad she wasn't with them, but figured she'd have a chance later.

After dinner they went to the lighthouse and summoned Brigid. They'd been at it for an hour and Cyl finally said, "I don't think she's coming tonight."

There was a knock on the table.

"Ah. I stand corrected."

"Sorry to bother you again so soon," said Luna. "But we just had one burning question for you. What was the name of the ship Aurnia was on?"

The pen hovered and Cyl held her breath. This was huge.

Lightning Spirit.

"Thank you," said Cyl.

"That's all we needed today. We'll let you rest now, okay?" Luna said. One knock.

"Good night, Brigid," said Martinique.

Cyl turned on the light.

"Time for more research."

"Yes," said Martinique. "Let's go look up *Lightning Spirit* and see what we can see."

"Shall I make drinks?" said Cyl.

"No. I need to drive home," said Martinique. "Unfortunately."

"No doubt," said Luna. "You'll be back though, right?"

"Just try and keep me out of your bed."

"Good answer."

"I found the ship," Martinique said. "But I don't know what date I'm looking for."

"Shit," said Cyl. "Oh, wait. I have her date of death in the family tree."

She pulled out the section on Aurnia, but it only had a year of death. No date.

"Damn," Cyl said. "I know it was in that book in the library. I'll swing by there tomorrow and look it up."

"Great," said Martinique. "I'll say good night then. I'll be back tomorrow night. Should I pack an overnight bag?"

"Please do," said Cyl.

"Great. See you both then."

The next day, Cyl was at the library racking her brain to try to remember which book they'd found the information on Aurnia. She sent Luna a text.

Sorry to bother you. Which book did we find out about Aurnia in?

Death records.

Ah, yes. Thanks.

She made her way to that section and was surprised to find Tawny there.

"Fancy meeting you here," Cyl said.

"Oh, hi. I'm just looking into things before work."

"What are you looking up?"

"Info on Aurnia."

"Same here," said Cyl. "Mind if I join you?"

"Not at all. I need to get going anyway. I'll see you later."

Something was off about Tawny, but Cyl couldn't put her finger on it. She felt like Tawny was deliberately avoiding them. But, why?

She settled into the book on death records and found the section on Aurnia Byrne. Aurnia had, in fact been off the coast of Hispaniola when she died. Cyl jotted the date in her phone and headed home.

It was hard to believe she'd been in Tampa for two months and still hadn't fixed up the cottage. She had work to do, but chasing down facts about Brigid and Aurnia was so much more fun.

What to do with the information she had? She searched for *Lightning Spirit* online and found a host of alcoholic beverages. She searched for *Lightning Spirit* boat and finally found some interesting information.

She found a website dedicated to the ship which was out of commission in the eighteen hundreds. She searched for Hispaniola and found that Tampa to Hispaniola had been a popular route for the ship.

Cyl put in the date of Aurnia's death and saw exactly where the ship had been. It was between Hispaniola and Cuba, though closer to Hispaniola. Which meant that Brigid's ship had to be in there somewhere as well.

She searched the website for *Tainted Rose*. She hit the jackpot. There was a whole page dedicated to the night *Lightning Spirit* came upon *Tainted Rose* as she went down. It even mentioned Brigid by name. Captain Brigid Doyle. Cyl was learning some valuable information. She was excited to share it with Luna and Martinique.

There was even a map showing exactly where the ship had come across *Tainted Rose*. Cyl had so much information and wasn't sure what to do with it. She had an idea though.

She opened a new tab and looked for organizations who searched for sunken treasure. There was quite a list, so she narrowed it down to Tampa based. She found three and was reading about the second one when she heard someone pull up on the driveway.

Cyl glanced at her watch. It was almost six. Martinique or Luna must be there. She opened the door and kissed Luna, then waited since Martinique was pulling in right behind her.

Martinique kissed both Luna and Cyl in such a way that left Cyl throbbing.

"So, are we a throuple now?" Luna said when they were all inside.

"A what?" said Cyl.

"A throuple," said Martinique. "It's like a couple but there are three of us."

"Seriously?"

"Seriously. I think we should try it," said Luna.

"I'm game," said Martinique.

"It seems I've been outvoted. But I can't complain. Two of you means double the fun."

"Exactly," said Luna.

"Tell us about your day," said Martinique. "After we get settled with some wine and maybe get a dinner order placed? I'm starved."

Cyl poured the wine and opened a beer. Martinique ordered dinner then they snuggled on the couch.

"I learned so much today."

"Did you? Like what?" said Luna.

Cyl went on to tell them every tidbit of information she'd uncovered.

"Damn," said Martinique. "You were busy."

"Indeed. And you'll never guess who I ran into again today?"

"Tawny?" said Luna.

"Bingo. She was reading over Aurnia's death notice. I think she's up to something."

"But what? She can't get any information from Brigid if she doesn't come to the séances. And she's not hanging around us so we can't share tidbits with her."

"True," said Cyl. "But it was like…I don't know. As soon as she saw me, she went pale as a ghost herself. And then she left right away. I don't know. It was weird."

"Sounds like it," said Luna. "So my question is, what do we do with this information?"

"Way ahead of you," said Cyl. "So I guess if we're a throuple or whatever, we need to make decisions together. But I've been looking for companies that specialize in finding sunken boats and therefore sunken treasures. I bet we could find Brigid's treasure and maybe what's left of Aurnia's body to bring back here."

"That would be amazing," said Luna.

"How much would all this cost?"

"I'm not that far yet, Martinique. Still just researching."

"I bet we could afford it," Luna said. "If we all pitched in."

"Possibly," said Martinique.

"What's holding you back?" Cyl said. "It's not just the money, is it?"

"No. I don't know why I'm hesitant, but I am. I'm also outvoted, so research away."

She kissed Cyl then. It was a kiss that made her toes curl. Cyl pulled her close and lost her head as their tongues tangoed. Until the doorbell rang.

"Don't mind me. I'll get it," said Luna.

They laughed and took a break for dinner, with Cyl just getting warmed up for later.

CHAPTER EIGHTEEN

Cyl decided which company she wanted to go with and made an appointment for the three of them to go meet with them the following Saturday. The idea had slowly grown on Martinique and even she was excited Friday night when they went to meet with Brigid.

Brigid seemed to be waiting for them. They'd barely said their summoning when there was a knock on the table.

"Are you in a good mood tonight, Brigid?" said Luna. One knock.

"We have exciting news for you," Martinique said. "We may just go in search of your treasure and Aurnia." One knock.

"You'd like that?" said Cyl.

The pen hovered briefly.

Aurnia.

"You want us to bring her home, don't you?" said Luna. One knock.

"Do you think you'd be at peace then?" said Martinique. One knock.

"We're going to do our best to make it happen," Cyl said. "We're meeting with a group tomorrow who specialize in finding sunken ships." One knock.

"Right?" said Luna. "We weren't sure we were all in agreement, but we are now."

"Yes, we are," Martinique beamed. Even in the darkness Cyl could see her smile and something inside her shifted.

"Just to make sure we're on the right path, is your last name Doyle?" Cyl forced her thoughts back to the matter at hand. One knock.

"Great. Yep," said Luna. "We have a pretty good idea of where you went down. And we think Aurnia is around there too." One knock.

"You agree? That's great. We can't wait to go in search of. We have such high hopes."

Martinique's excitement was palpable. Cyl, already hyped about the adventure, was enjoying it all the more since the rest of her throuple were on board.

"So you met Aurnia off the coast of Hispaniola, right?" Luna seemed to be all business. One knock.

"And you had a torrid affair for two weeks?" Martinique said.

The pen hovered again.

Injured.

"Right," said Cyl. "How torrid could the affair be with you dying and all?"

"Was Aurnia sick at that time?" said Martinique. One knock.

"But you still fell in love and knew she was the one for you," Luna stated it, rather than asking. One knock.

"Wow." Martinique leaned back in her seat while still holding Cyl's and Luna's hands. "How sad." One knock.

"And after you died, you came here to meet up with her, but she died out there and you've been here waiting ever since?" Cyl said. One knock.

"I sure hope we can bring her home for you," said Luna. One knock.

The pen hovered.

Tired.

"Okay," said Cyl. "We'll be back tomorrow night to tell you about the ship hunters." One knock.

"Good night," Martinique and Luna said in unison.

Cyl flipped the switch, blew out the candles, and wrapped her arms around her lovers.

"Bedtime?" she said.

"I need to decompress," said Luna. "You two can get started. I'll join you in a bit."

"You sure you're okay with that?" said Cyl.

"I'm fine. She's part of us. You didn't mind last week when we showered together."

"True. Okay. I'm just usure of all the rules and whatnot."

"Not any rules that don't apply to a regular relationship. There are just more people to play with."

"Sounds good to me," Cyl said. She took Martinique's hand and led her to the bedroom. Martinique was always fun, but one-on-one, she was a special kind of enjoyment. Cyl tried to take Martinique's blouse off, but once she got it over her chest, Martinique objected.

"That's far enough."

Cyl was confused but undaunted. Then her mind drifted back to her first encounter with Martinique. Martinique hadn't undressed then either.

She lifted Martinique's bra above her breasts and looked into Martinique's eyes.

"That can't feel good."

"Au contraire. It feels dirty. Like we're sneaking."

"Suit yourself. Am I allowed to slip those shorts off?"

"Now, what do you think?"

Cyl laughed then slid her hand down Martinique's shorts. She found her hot and wet and ready. Cyl squeezed her own legs together to alleviate some of the pressure. It didn't help.

She sucked and tugged Martinique's nipple while she thrust her fingers as deep as she could.

"My clit," said Martinique. "Holy shit. Rub my clit and get me off."

Happy to oblige, Cyl was grateful she didn't have neighbors when Martinique loudly found her release.

"Your turn," said Martinique. Cyl stripped under the disapproving stare.

"Sorry. I need to be naked."

"And there's nothing wrong with that." Luna walked in leaving a trail of clothes behind her. Martinique got naked then and they all lay together on the bed.

"Lie back, Cyl. You do so much for us. You just lie back and close your eyes," said Luna.

Cyl was happy to oblige. The idea of both of them making her come appealed to her in a big way. She lay on her back and closed her eyes.

Luna licked her inner thighs, stopping just before hitting the money zone. Cyl knew it was Luna because she loved to tease. Martinique licked and sucked her nipples, driving her closer and closer to the edge.

Cyl felt Luna's tongue inside her and on her as she sucked her lower lips. She sensed movement and opened her eyes to see Martinique lowering herself onto Cyl's face.

"Fuck yeah," Cyl said as she moved her whole face against Martinique's wetness. She focused her mouth on Martinique while Luna continued to work her magic on Cyl's pussy. The sensations were too much and Cyl missed a few steps with Martinique when she rode her own orgasm to new heights.

Martinique followed close behind and she and Cyl turned their attention to Luna, who was a wet mess by then. Cyl's fingers and tongue played in and out of Luna until Luna screamed like a banshee as she shot into oblivion.

Saturday morning, they lounged in bed, trading sexual favors for errands. They wanted Cyl to start the coffee, so Luna had to suck Cyl's nipple while Martinique stroked her. Then Martinique wanted the paper so she pleased Luna to go get it.

It was an enjoyable way to pass the morning for sure. But soon it was time for showers and to go to Pirate's Booty.

A dark-haired man with a five o'clock shadow at one in the afternoon came out when they walked in.

"I'm Bruce," he said. "And you are?"

"I'm Cyl. We spoke on the phone about possible treasure buried off the coast of Hispaniola?"

"Ah yeah. Gotcha. Popular spot. Another lady was in here this morning asking about it."

"Was that other lady a cute strawberry blonde?"

Bruce nodded.

"Indeed she was."

"Tawny!" said Martinique.

"We need to get there before her," said Cyl.

"Easy does it. We haven't discussed anything yet. And she couldn't afford our services anyway. Now won't you come in and have a seat?"

He led them into a lovely office with royal blue plush carpeting and black leather furniture. Bruce, or whoever Bruce worked for, obviously did quite well for themselves.

"Would you like some coffee? Or perhaps champagne?" said Bruce.

"Coffee now," Cyl said. "Champagne if we make a deal."

"Fair enough." Bruce served them each a cup of coffee then settled back in his chair. "Tell me. What do you need from me?"

"We need someone to take us to the Dominican Republic. We have reason to believe there's treasure buried there."

"Are you experienced divers?"

They shook their heads.

"So you'll need a diver on board." It was a statement, not a question.

"How do we know we can trust you?" said Luna.

"We're licensed and bonded. We also dive with cameras so you can see exactly what we're looking at at all times."

Martinique and Luna looked at Cyl who nodded.

"Okay. How liable are we if something goes wrong to the diver?"

"You're not. We're doing this at our risk."

"I want that in writing."

"And you shall have it."

"What's the cost?" said Martinique.

"Well, there's the rental of the boat and the fuel to get there and back. It should take about fourteen hours or so. Then there's the diver. And our standard fee."

"Which amounts to what?" said Cyl.

"Seventy-five hundred."

"Yikes," said Martinique.

"May we speak in private, please?" said Cyl.

"Of course. I'll be right outside."

With Bruce out of sight, Cyl looked at Luna and Martinique.

"That's only twenty-five hundred apiece. We should be able to swing that. Think of how far we've come."

"She's right," said Luna. "I can afford my share. I just need to arrange to be away from the studio."

They looked at Martinique.

"Fine," she said. "I'll make it work."

Cyl called Bruce back in.

"We're in," she said. "When can we make this happen?"

"Let me check our schedule." He opened a laptop and clicked. "We should be able to do it in a month."

"There's nothing sooner?" said Luna. "Check. Maybe next week?"

Bruce clicked some more.

"Would you settle for the week after?"

"Perfect," Cyl said. "That'll give you two time to get work figured out."

"We'll need half the payment before we take off and the other half when we get back."

"Fair enough."

They talked details and Cyl left feeling like she was going to Disneyland. They were going on a huge adventure. Like nothing they'd ever done before. It was really happening.

That night they told Brigid about their plans.

"So it's all set. It's going to happen. Are you okay with this?" One knock.

"Great," said Luna. "We're excited."

The pen hovered.

Aurnia?

"Yes," said Martinique. "We'll look for Aurnia as well." One knock.

"We kind of left that part out," said Cyl. "I'll call Bruce Monday."

She turned her attention back to Brigid.

"Is there anything in particular you want us to save? Any trinket we should keep our eyes open for?" Two knocks.

"You want it all, don't you?" said Luna. One knock.

"You got it," said Cyl. "We'll bring back what we find."

They chatted for a little while longer until Brigid claimed tiredness and Cyl was happy to get back to the cottage and start making plans.

"So you two need to get your time off from work. A few days should do it. But I'd take a week to be safe."

"What about you, Cyl?" said Martinique. "What happened to a few months here, sell the place, and move back to Colorado?"

"Let's not talk about that right now. I honestly don't know what I'm doing."

"Well, that's better than a definite, 'I'm leaving,'" said Luna.

"Yes. I suppose it is," said Martinique.

"I wonder if we can fish on the boat," said Cyl.

"Not to change the subject or anything," said Martinique.

"Right?" Luna said.

"I'm just thinking out loud. I've never been deep sea fishing. I bet it would be a rush."

"So would staying in Tampa," said Martinique.

"I said I didn't want to talk about it right now."

"Then when?" said Martinique.

"I don't know. But right now we have more pressing matters to pursue."

"I'm so glad we found Brigid," said Luna.

"As am I," Cyl said.

"Yes," said Martinique. "She brought us together."

"That she did," said Cyl.

"And what a great thing that's been," Luna said.

"Indeed."

"So what shall we do for the rest of the night?" said Martinique.

"Get stupid drunk and have an orgy." Luna laughed.

"That's my girl," Cyl said.

"And I'm your girl, too. Though I prefer the term, woman."

"I mean no disrespect to Luna when I call her my girl. Nor to you."

"I appreciate that. Now let's drink. Or we could fast-forward to the orgy."

"I'll pour the wine and I'll have a bourbon."

"Don't get too drunk. We need you awake," Martinique said.

"Oh. So stupid drunk isn't going to happen?"

"You do what you want," said Martinique. "If you pass out, Luna and I will keep each other entertained."

"I don't doubt that." Cyl opened a beer. "I don't doubt that for a minute."

Chapter Nineteen

The next week flew by, and it was time to board the boat for the Caribbean. Cyl was excited but nervous. What if they didn't find Brigid's treasure? Or worse, what if they didn't find Aurnia? That was going to be the greater challenge. One dead body in the middle of the sea? What were the chances?

She'd already considered the fact that Aurnia might have washed ashore centuries before. If only they knew how to find out for certain. But she couldn't let herself ponder that for long. She'd have to trust that they'd find Aurnia. They'd find her and bring her home to Brigid. Where she belonged.

The boat they were on was more like a yacht. It was for luxury cruising and the women enjoyed the champagne and shrimp cocktail as they set sail. It would be a long day with nothing to see but open water. But Cyl had been promised fishing so she was excited. And there was plenty of space to get inside and out of the sun if need arose.

They'd been on the water a couple of hours and Cyl could tell Martinique was getting restless.

"You okay?" Cyl asked her.

"Yeah. It's just hard to bask in the sun when you can't get in the water to cool off, you know?"

"True statement."

"I know something fun we could do inside," said Luna.

"What's that?"

"Let's find an empty stateroom."

"Luna!" said Martinique.

"Why not? Cyl? Are you up for it?"

"Sure. I'm always up for it. You know that."

"Great. Cyl and I will see you later."

"I'm coming," said Martinique.

"You will be soon," Luna said.

Cyl opened the door to her suite. It had a king-sized bed, a couch, coffee table and television. Not to mention the mini fridge and desk.

"These rooms are so nice," said Martinique. "I could get used to this life."

"How about we get out of our clothes?" Cyl was aroused and saw no reason to prolong the inevitable.

"How about we don't?" said Martinique. "What if someone walks in?"

"I locked the door," Cyl said. "No one is going to walk in on us. What is it with you and sex in clothes?"

"It's a fetish," Martinique said.

"I think it's kind of cool," said Luna. "It makes me feel nasty to keep some clothes on while we fuck."

"Seriously?" Cyl shook her head. "It's frustrating. But you both know I'd never deny you so you make the call. Let me know how this is going to play out."

"I want to tie you up and devour your delicious body," said Martinique.

"Too bad we don't have any scarves."

"But you have shorts," said Luna.

"Oh. I like the way you're thinking," said Martinique. "Okay. On the bed, stud."

Cyl lay on the bed and watched as Martinique and Luna removed each other's suits. If Cyl had such a thing as a fetish, it would be topless women. They drove her crazy. Luna was naked, but Martinique still had her bottoms on. She was fucking hot. Cyl knew she'd have to work to get Martinique off, but it would be worth it.

She watched as the other two apparently forgot she was there and got into a heavy make out session with each other. They were moaning and groaning and hands were roaming and Cyl felt like someone had turned the faucet on between her legs.

Cyl cleared her throat but didn't get their attention. They finally came up for air a few minutes later.

"Did you two forget about me?" Cyl said.

"Oh, my God." Luna straddled Cyl's face. "I need you to finish me off, stud."

Cyl was happy to oblige. She feasted on Luna as if she were the only woman on earth. She licked and sucked and licked some more. Luna rewarded Cyl by flooding her face with the evidence of her orgasm.

Martinique had been watching and when Cyl looked over at her, she had her hand down her bottoms.

"Get over here," said Cyl. "That's mine."

Luna cleaned Martinique's fingers while Cyl used her fingers to take Martinique over the edge. The women looked down at Cyl, still completely dressed and smiled.

"You look like you're about to self-combust," said Luna.

"Something like that," Cyl said.

Martinique pulled Cyl's board shorts down to her knees then bent and took Cyl in her mouth. Cyl wanted to spread her legs wider, to let Martinique really have at her, but she couldn't move her legs.

Martinique had her close. She could feel the heat coiling in her center. Just a few more strokes and she'd be there. Oh, God, she was beyond ready.

There was a knock on the door.

"Cyl? If you want to fish, you'd better get topside."

"On my way," Cyl called back.

Shit. So much for that much needed orgasm. Oh well. The knock on the door had pretty much been like a bucket of ice.

"Are you two coming?" Cyl got her clothes on right.

"You're the only one who didn't." Luna laughed.

"Very funny. I'll see you two up there."

She found the crewmember named Tommy waiting for her at the back of the boat.

"You think you can handle this?" he said.

"Heck yeah. I was born for this."

"Excellent. Here's your bait. Your rig is all set up. Slap some bait on and give it a whirl."

"How much time do we have?" said Cyl.

"We have a couple of hours. Maybe a little longer. Long enough to let you take your best shot."

Cyl cast her line as far as she could then sat in a padded chair. This boat had all the comforts. And she loved it.

"So we don't have any beer?" she said.

"I'll have Harv bring us some."

Harv showed up with a bucket of Coronas and limes. Oh yeah. Cyl never wanted this trip to end. The other two showed up and sat in the other chairs.

"Where are the real drinks?" said Luna.

"What would you ladies like?"

"I feel like if we're in the Caribbean, we should be drinking piña coladas."

"Oh. Good call, babe," said Martinique.

"I'll text Harv again. You two beauties just relax."

If Tommy had thought it weird that Martinique had called Luna babe, he didn't show it. Tommy seemed to take everything in stride. And Cyl appreciated that.

Cyl was feeling good. The sun, the water, the women, and the beer had lulled her into a deep state of relaxation. She'd thrown her line out three times and every time she'd reeled it in, the bait was missing. So something was down there.

She was just about to close her eyes when her pole bent nearly in half. She jumped up, set the hook and began to reel it in. Or try to. She thought she was in good shape. She thought she was strong. But, damn! Whatever was on the other end was determined to make her work for it.

"Easy there, Turbo," said Tommy. "Don't fight so hard. Let it wear itself out."

"Seriously? Where's the challenge?"

"Trust me. There'll be plenty of challenge."

Cyl kept her eyes on where the water was moving and saw something break the surface. She couldn't tell what it was. It was blue but didn't look like a fish. Then it jumped. And Cyl saw the most stunning sailfish she could imagine.

Forty-five minutes later, Cyl's arms felt like mush.

"You ready to bring her in?"

"I guess so."

Tommy flipped a switch and the line started reeling itself in.

"This was motorized this whole time?" Cyl wasn't amused.

"Sure was." Tommy grinned. "But you had to manually fight it. Sorry."

"Whatever."

"You going to want to mount this?" Tommy said.

"Let it go," said Luna. "It would be cruel to keep it."

"I want it. I'm going to mount it," said Cyl.

"Keeping trophies as well as women. Why am I not surprised?" Martinique said.

Once the fish was landed, Tommy took pictures of Cyl with it, then took it away to keep it until Cyl could get it mounted.

"I need a nap now," said Cyl. "I'm going to my room for a few."

"We'll go with," said Luna.

They got back to the room and Martinique insisted Cyl take a shower.

"You stink. Like beer and sweat and fish. And it's not attractive."

"I can't take a shower. My arms don't work."

"I'll join you," Martinique said.

"Fine. But no funny business. I'm telling you, I'm wiped."

"Fair enough."

"You two hurry," said Luna.

Cyl let the hot water pummel her sore shoulders. It felt really good.

"I think I can handle it," she told Martinique.

"Okay. I'll see you in the bedroom."

Cyl noticed Martinique didn't bother to get dressed and wondered if she and Luna were going to have some fun while Cyl slept. The thought woke up parts of her that she thought would remain dormant for a little longer. Suddenly she wanted her women. Desperately.

She dried off and stepped into the bedroom where she found Luna and Martinique cuddling naked. Hot damn. She was a lucky woman to have two such stunning lovers.

"I can't believe you two naked beauties are simply holding each other. I thought for sure I'd find some hanky-panky going on."

"We're waiting until you're up for it." Luna rolled onto her back. Her legs were spread wide and whether or not it was intentional, it made Cyl's mouth water.

"I'm up for it," said Cyl. "Although I don't know if my hands will work."

"Lucky for us you've got a talented mouth," said Martinique.

Cyl grinned and relaxed as Luna kissed her passionately while Martinique sucked a nipple. Cyl's nipple stood at attention at the feel of Martinique's tongue, and she knew whoever touched her would find her wet and ready.

It was Martinique who dragged her hand down Cyl's body to where her legs met.

"Damn. Someone's worked up."

"Fuck me, Martinique. No talking."

Martinique plunged her fingers in deep, just how Cyl liked it. She withdrew them, added another finger, and thrust inside her again.

"Oh, fuck yeah," said Cyl. "That's what I'm talkin' about."

Luna moved down to between Cyl's legs. She licked and sucked Cyl's clit while Martinique seemed to go deeper every time.

Cyl's arms may have been like oatmeal, but her hips worked just fine. She arched up and gyrated, forcing Martinique to hit all her favorite spots. She did manage to hold Luna's head in place as well, so Luna's talented tongue never missed a beat.

"Holy fuck, I'm going to come," said Cyl. "Oh, holy shit. Dear God. Oh, Fuck yes!" She screamed loudly as she rode the crescendo until she gently floated back down. "Damn, what you two do to me."

"That was fun," said Luna.

"Mm-hm. And now I'm super horny.

"You two take care of each other. I'll watch."

"On one condition," said Luna.

"What's that?"

"You touch yourself when we get you horny again."

Cyl thought about it. Where was the harm in it? She doubted her arms would let her, but it was worth promising.

"You got it."

She lay there listening to the sounds of Martinique's and Luna's wet pussies as fingers maneuvered in and out of each other. She watched the pleasure on their faces and figured what the hell?

She reached between her legs and gently circled her clit. She felt it swell to almost bursting and she began rubbing it faster as she watched her two women near their breaking point.

Oh, shit. She was going to come again. She had to hold out. Couldn't come before they did. Fortunately, Luna yelled out just before Martinique found her release so Cyl let herself soar into orbit yet again.

Damn. Life was good. Like, really good. She'd never had this much fun before. Would it be worth staying in Tampa? Really, what was for her in Fort Collins except her business? And she could open a business up here.

She was thinking crazy thoughts. Tampa wasn't her home. Sure, she was having fun, but would it last? Could it?

CHAPTER TWENTY

The sun wasn't up yet when there was a pounding on Cyl's door. She pulled on shorts and a T-shirt and answered.

"We're just of the coast of the Dominican Republic. We need you up top."

"Oh, great. Let me wake the other two and we'll be up."

She grabbed her phone and called Martinique then Luna, relaying the message. Both women promised to be there shortly. Cyl slid her phone in her pocket and went up to the deck.

"Coffee?" said Harv.

"Dear God, yes," Cyl said. "Please and thank you."

Tommy walked up, decked out in a wetsuit.

"Shouldn't we wait until the sun comes up?" said Cyl.

"Where we're diving? It's never seen the sun so it doesn't matter."

"I suppose that's true."

Martinique and Luna showed up looking like they could have used a few more hours of sleep. Cyl grinned. They were so adorable.

"Harv's got coffee," Cyl said.

"Thank God."

"So we've studied the map you gave us and this is where it seems to be. Three of us will dive. We'll all have cameras and lights. The TV is just above the bar. You'll be able to see everything we're doing," said Tommy.

"Excellent." Cyl was getting more excited by the minute.

"We can't promise you we'll find anything," Tommy said. "But we're sure as hell going to try."

"Appreciate that."

"Any questions," said Tommy.

"Please be careful," said Luna. "I have an uneasy feeling about this."

"We're always careful. See you on TV."

The three divers entered the water. The sea life was amazing to watch.

"We need to get our scuba licenses," said Cyl.

"In your dreams. You couldn't pay me enough," said Luna.

"Are you afraid of the water?" said Martinique. "Because I'm with Cyl."

"I'm not afraid of the water per se. I don't know. Scuba diving just freaks me out."

"Fair enough." Cyl hugged her. "You do you, babe."

"Thank you."

Cyl turned her attention back to the TV where the divers were still heading down. Harv kept their mugs full and had set out cream and sugar on the bar. He also put out some Danishes for them to enjoy while they waited.

The sun was up, and the divers had surfaced three times and dove four yet still they simply swam along the sea bottom. Nothing noticeable had been found. Cyl was about to give up when one of the divers held up a faded painted plank. Cyl stared at the screen trying to figure out what the picture was on the cloth. It was a rose outlined in black.

"The *Tainted Rose*," said Cyl.

Martinique and Luna had been dozing in lawn chairs. They hurried to the bar when they heard Cyl.

"Oh, my God. It is," said Martinique.

"Radio to them to keep that," said Cyl.

Harv did as he was asked. They all watched in rapt attention as the divers swam on. Soon, the cameras showed an old wooden ship. Luna squeezed Cyl's hand and Cyl smiled. This was really happening. They swam in and around the different parts of the ship.

One of them swam into what appeared to be the hull. A collective gasp went up at the bar when they saw the chest of gold and jewels.

"Holy shit! We found it!" said Cyl.

The diver gave a thumbs up and the three of them swam upward.

"You wanted this?" Tommy handed Cyl what was left of the *Tainted Rose*'s flag.

Cyl got goose bumps as she held the tattered remains of Brigid's flag. Luna and Martinique huddled close to her.

"I can't believe we found it," said Luna.

"No kidding," Martinique said. "This is awesome. It's a truly awesome surprise."

"That it is," said Cyl. "I really can't thank you guys enough."

"Always a pleasure," said Tommy. "This is a treat for us, too. Y'all need to remember that."

"I'm glad," said Luna.

"So how do we get the treasure up?" Cyl said.

"We'll get there. We'll go back down in just a few. And we'll haul it up. No worries. What are y'all going to do with all that? You'll be filthy rich. You split it three ways and you'll still be stinkin' rich."

"We haven't really talked about that yet. I suppose we should though," said Cyl.

"Yeah, you should. That's quite a treasure."

"We'll have to declare it or something, won't we?"

"I think you need to make sure no museum wants it or something like that," said Tommy. "I'm not sure about that though."

"Thanks. We'll definitely look into that," Cyl said.

When the chest was lowered onto the deck, the men stepped away and gave them their time with it.

"This is amazing," said Cyl. "Brigid is going to be so happy."

"What *are* we going to do with it all?" Martinique said.

"Who knows? Sell it and invest? Bury it in my yard?" Cyl laughed. "We'll figure it out."

Upon closer inspection, the chest contained lots of coins and lots of jewelry. And plenty of gold bars. Brigid had truly amassed a fortune in her time on the water. The men had also brought up sabers and pistols and other weapons.

Cyl felt uncomfortable looking through all this that clearly belonged to Brigid. She almost felt like she could see Brigid in action. As if hundreds of years hadn't passed between her living days and today. It was disconcerting and she stepped back.

She rested her forearms on the railing and gazed out to sea. She saw a speck on the horizon.

"Tommy? What's that?"

Tommy used his binoculars.

"Looks like another boat. Although why anybody would be out here is beyond me. It's really moving too. Looks like they're in a hurry."

Who would be out there in a boat besides them? Cyl could only think of one person. Tawny. Cyl grinned. A little too little. A little too late.

"Let's get out of here," she said. "We don't want trouble."

"No one says they're trouble. Just some boaters who are lost."

"Or looking for this treasure."

"What?"

"Cyl, what are you talking about?" said Martinique.

"We all know that Tawny tried to charter this boat, but couldn't afford it. Who else would be on a boat out here?"

"I think you're being paranoid," said Luna.

"I hope I am. But I don't think so. Tommy, can I use your eyes?"

The boat was very close at that point. Close enough that through the binoculars, Cyl could easily make out Tawny standing on deck.

"You didn't believe me?" said Cyl. "Here. Take a look."

Luna took the binoculars and gasped.

"Holy shit."

"Exactly. I don't know what she's willing to do to get this treasure, but we need to get out of here."

"But there's more down there," said Tommy.

"Not much. Let her have it. Let's go. They're practically on top of us."

Tommy radioed the captain to take off and they did. He gunned it so fast that Cyl and Luna and Martinique ended up in a pile on the deck.

"You three okay?" Tommy said.

"I am. How about you two?" Cyl got to her feet and quickly sat in a deck chair.

"I'm fine."

"So am I."

"Good," said Cyl. "Now let's just get as far away as possible."

"So we're heading toward Cuba," said Tommy. "Any chance that boat will meet us there?"

"Doubtful," said Cyl. "She's after the treasure. She couldn't care less about Aurnia's body."

"Should we be afraid? Like is there a danger of violence?"

"I don't think so," said Luna. "She may be obsessed and secretive, but I don't think she's violent."

"Good. It doesn't look like they're following us at any rate," said Tommy.

"That's a relief," said Martinique.

"You three sure you're okay?"

"Yes," said Martinique. "But I could use a cocktail."

"Coming right up," said Tommy. "Beer, Cyl?"

"I'll have a piña colada as well, thanks."

Tommy texted Harv and shortly three cocktails arrived. Cyl took a sip.

"Damn. That'll put hair on your chest," she said.

"Oh, shit. That's strong," said Luna.

"I figured you ladies needed that," said Harv.

"We do. Thanks. And expect to make more as the day wears on," said Cyl.

The moon was high when Tommy approached Cyl, who was barely conscious.

"We think we're at the spot," he said. "You ready?"

"Oh shit," she slurred. "Yeah. You bet I'm ready."

Harv showed up with a large coffee for Cyl.

"I thought this might help," he said.

"Thanks."

The other two were passed out cold in their chairs. Cyl debated letting them sleep, but thought they'd probably want to witness this.

They woke and gratefully accepted their coffees from Harv.

"What are our chances?" said Martinique. "Like seriously, Tommy. She was buried at sea four hundred years ago."

"Well, I can tell you the chances of her remaining in the place she went overboard are slim and none. The currents would have moved her who knows where. And then, who's to say she hasn't already washed up? She could be a Jane Doe buried in Cuba for all we know."

"That's what I was afraid of."

"Besides, have you got dental records? Something we can be sure we have the right body with?"

"No." Luna sounded so forlorn.

"Look," said Cyl. "Maybe we don't find her. And if not, it's okay. The point is, we made a promise to try and that's what we're doing."

Cyl sat at the end of the bar and focused on the television while the divers went down once again.

"God, I hope we find her," she said.

"It would be the icing on the cake," said Martinique.

"Yeah, it would."

"I don't think I want this coffee," Luna said. "I think I'll head to bed."

"And miss the excitement? Are you okay?" Cyl said.

"I'm fine. Just tired. And don't want to be up anymore. Wake me up if we find her, please."

"Will do."

"I hope she's all right," said Martinique.

"Me, too. Of all of us, I would expect her to be the most excited."

"Same here."

"Maybe she's feeling sick. We did have a lot to drink."

"True."

Tommy and the other divers surfaced for the fifth time. Having been following along on the television, Cyl knew better than to ask if they'd found anything.

"We're going to move a little east," Tommy said. "According to our calculations that's the way the current would have carried her. But again, I make no promises."

"Understood." Cyl was feeling more despondent by the minute. Sure, Brigid would be thrilled they'd gotten the treasure and the flag, but it was Aurnia she wanted.

The sun was cresting when the gang surfaced for the final time.

"Sorry," said Tommy.

"That's okay," said Cyl. "We knew it was a wild goose chase."

"It really was. But I was really hoping to find this woman you're looking for."

"We'll have to fly to Havana and check the list of Jane Does there."

"That could make for an exciting trip," said Martinique. "But for now, I'm exhausted. I'll see everyone in the morning."

"I guess I'd better get some shut eye, too. And you guys must be exhausted as well."

"I'm high on adrenaline," said Tommy. "But we'll go below soon enough."

"Thanks for everything, Tommy. We really appreciate it."

"It was our pleasure."

Cyl's room was unlocked when she arrived, which was a good thing because she couldn't remember where she'd left her key. She went into the bedroom and found Luna sound asleep. She must have had Cyl's key.

Luna rolled over as Cyl undressed.

"Well?" she said.

"No luck."

"I knew that was going to happen. That's why I went to bed. I couldn't handle the disappointment."

"How'd you know we'd be disappointed?"

"Just a feeling I had. I'm crushed. Absolutely crushed. I so wanted to find Aurnia and bring her home."

"I know, babe. We're all devastated. But we have a plan."

"We do?"

"Rest well, lover. I'll tell you about it in the morning."

CHAPTER TWENTY-ONE

They got the treasure chest into the lighthouse as soon as they got home. It wasn't easy and took all three of them to carry it. But they got it in then waited for dark to come.

Brigid had obviously seen the chest before they got there. Jewels and coins were strewn about and the painted plank was missing. Cyl took the stairs up to the gallery and found the plank on one of the chairs there. She brought it back down then they turned off the light and summoned Brigid.

"I see you found your treasure," said Luna. One knock.

"Are you happy we found it?" Martinique said. One knock.

"That's great. We've been pretty excited," Luna said.

"What do you want us to do with all of it?" said Cyl.

The pen hovered.

Yours now.

"You don't want us to bury it or something?" Cyl said. Two knocks.

Keep it.

"Thank you, Brigid," said Martinique. "Thank you so much."

"Yeah. We weren't sure what you'd want but had to ask," said Cyl.

The pen hovered again.

Aurnia?

"We're sorry, Brigid," said Martinique. "We tried. We really did."

The pen flew across the room. Coins were tossed everywhere. The light came on then went off again. Clearly, Brigid was unhappy.

"Brigid?" Luna said. "Calm down. Let's talk." Two loud knocks.

"Would you like us to leave?" said Cyl. One loud knock.

"Okay," said Martinique. "But we'll be back another night." Two loud knocks.

"Yes, we will," Luna said. "But not for a while."

They got back to the cottage where Cyl could see Luna's red, splotched face and swollen eyes. She pulled her into a tight hug.

"It's okay, babe. She needs to process it."

"We failed," said Luna. "We let her down."

"Not for lack of trying," said Martinique.

"Did we though? Did we do everything we could?"

"We did," Cyl said. "And soon we'll fly to Havana and look up records for bodies that washed ashore. It's not over yet. I refuse to admit defeat."

"I love that about you, Cyl. I wish I could feel your optimism," said Luna.

"Let's book our flights," said Martinique. "Let's fly out for a weekend, so Luna and I don't have to take more time off work."

"Sounds good."

Cyl pulled up flights from Tampa to Havana. They were pretty darned cheap. She booked their flights for two weeks out.

"Thanks, Cyl," said Luna. "I hope two days will be enough."

"So do I. And if it's not, you two can fly home and I'll extend my stay."

"You would do that?" Luna said.

"I would. I want to find Aurnia as bad as you two do. Believe me."

"And what happens if we find her?" said Martinique.

"We get permission to bring her home. I want her buried on my property."

"And when you sell this place?" Luna said.

"One day at a time," said Cyl. "One day at a time."

"So you don't deny you still plan to sell?" Martinique said.

"I haven't made up my mind. I'm not crazy about the weather here, but you two are here and I don't know what's important enough in Fort Collins to make me go back. But, my mind isn't made up."

"At least you're honest about not seeing a future with us," said Luna.

"What did I just say? Don't you dare twist my words."

"I'm going to bed," Luna said. "I'm afraid I'm not very good company tonight."

"Okay," said Martinique. "I'm sure we'll be in shortly."

"You two should make love," said Luna. "Someone should be able to have some fun tonight."

Cyl laughed.

"If the mood strikes, we will. I promise."

"Thanks."

"You want something to drink?" Cyl said.

"I'd love a glass of wine."

"Want to go up to the gallery and watch the gulf?"

"I'd rather go sit at the point. Let's take a blanket and the bottle of wine."

"And the six-pack." Cyl began putting things together.

They walked out to the point and spread the blanket. They sat down and sipped their drinks and enjoyed the quiet night.

"It's so beautiful out here," said Martinique. "Just gorgeous."

"It really is. It's a beautiful night and I've got a beautiful woman next to me. What more could I want?"

"You're such a charmer."

"But I mean it."

"I know you do. But still, you have a way with words."

"That's because I have a talented tongue." Cyl laughed.

"Remind me."

Cyl kissed Martinique. It was an open-mouthed kiss and she stroked her tongue over Martinique's. Over, under, and around, until their breathing got heavy.

"Holy fuck," said Martinique. "You're going to have to fuck me now."

"Here?"

"Here. I need that tongue to get me off."

Martinique lay back on the blanket and slid her shorts off. She spread her legs and looked at Cyl with passion burning in her eyes.

"Tongue only?" Cyl said.

"You can use those talented fingers, too."

Cyl moved between Martinique's legs and gazed upon her shiny pink flesh. She buried her face in Martinique's pussy and lapped and sucked her lips and clit.

"Shit yes," said Martinique. "Oh, God, yes."

Cyl buried her fingers deep inside Martinique while her lips and tongue paid special attention to her clit. Martinique pressed her hand to the back of Cyl's head and Cyl thought if she had to suffocate, this would be the way to go.

Martinique cried out and Cyl grinned to herself. She had a wonderful life here in Tampa. So why didn't she just commit to staying?

"How are you doing?" Martinique said when she'd found her voice.

"I'm hot and bothered."

"Take your shorts off."

"I'm afraid I'm not the exhibitionist you are."

"No one can see," said Martinique. "Live dangerously."

Against her better judgment, Cyl took off her shorts. The gulf breeze caressed her, but it was Martinique she wanted.

"See?" Martinique said. "It's nice isn't it?"

"Am I just going to lie here on display or are you going to do something?"

"You're so impatient. I'm going to make you beg for more."

"I don't doubt it," said Cyl.

Martinique set up camp between Cyl's legs.

"You're so fuckin' hot," Martinique said. "Like I don't know where to start."

"Start somewhere or I'm going to get myself off. Out here for everyone to see."

"Ooh. That could be fun. Mutual masturbation."

"Martinique?"

"Fine."

Martinique licked the length of Cyl then thrust her fingers deep. She knew just how Cyl liked it and Cyl responded. She was moaning and groaning and creeping closer and closer to the edge.

Martinique used her fingers on Cyl's clit and Cyl catapulted off the edge and into oblivion.

"I want more," said Martinique.

"Oh you do, do you?"

"Lie down here so you can see me."

Cyl moved so her head was by Martinique's feet. She watched as Martinique fingered herself and rubbed her clit.

"I'm so fucking wet, Cyl. Join me? Touch yourself?"

Cyl couldn't deny Martinique. They watched each other play with themselves until they cried out together.

"That was hot," said Martinique. "You have no idea how fuckin' sexy it is to see your fingers fucking yourself."

"You're pretty hot to watch, too."

"Thanks."

"Oh, believe me. It's my pleasure."

"We should get back to the cottage," said Martinique.

"Yeah. I could use some sleep."

They got dressed, walked back to the cottage, and climbed into bed.

"I smell sex," Luna said sleepily.

"It was your idea." Martinique laughed.

Luna smiled and drifted back to sleep.

Cyl was having strange erotic dreams. She was in a graveyard surrounded by ghosts who stripped her and were having their way with her. She woke with a start to find Luna between her legs and Martinique sucking her nipple.

"Holy shit," she said. "What a way to wake up. Good morning to me."

That was all she could say though as she was quickly made incoherent. Luna and Martinique definitely knew what they were doing and in no time, she cried out as she found her release.

"To what do I owe that pleasure?" Cyl said.

"You were too sexy lying there, so we had to do something about it," said Luna.

"Well, thank you. Now, who shall I do next?"

"We've already taken care of each other," said Martinique. "So the question is, what shall we do with this day?"

"I vote we stay in bed," Cyl said.

"Vetoed." Luna laughed. "Let's go to St. Pete."

"Oh yeah. Let's go to the beach," said Martinique.

"Sounds good to me."

They drove Mabel and parked in a safe lot. They walked down close to the water and set up their space. Cyl was lucky enough to get to apply sunscreen to both her women and doing so got her all hot and bothered again. There were too many people around to do anything about it though. She vowed to give them an experience they'd never forget when they got home.

"Let's get in the water," said Martinique.

They went as deep as they could without Martinique being over her head. She was the shortest, but the water was at her shoulders so they stopped. They bobbed and dove and overall enjoyed themselves.

Martinique looked like she was struggling with something underwater.

"Are you okay?" said Cyl.

"I need your help." Martinique took Cyl's hand and placed it between her legs. She'd dropped her bottoms and Cyl found warm, wet flesh.

"Oh, shit yeah," said Cyl.

She used her fingers to coax one after another orgasm out of Martinique, who held on to Cyl's shoulders so she didn't drown.

"My turn," said Luna.

Cyl pulled Luna's crotch off to the side while Martinique got herself put back together. Cyl finger-fucked Luna until Luna claimed to have nothing left.

Just as Luna cried out the last time, Martinique managed to get her hand down Cyl's shorts and stroked her clit until Cyl closed her eyes and held in a massive moan as she came.

The day passed with them alternating between laying out and swimming. Cyl was thoroughly relaxed by the time Martinique's stomach growled.

"Time for lunch?" said Cyl. She checked her watch. It was four thirty. "Or dinner, I guess?"

"Let's go home and change," said Luna. "I'm buying dinner. What do we want?"

"A steak," said Cyl.

"As usual." Laughed Martinique.

Martinique volunteered to shower in the outside shower, leaving Cyl and Luna to the one in the cottage. Luna had such a fantastic body. She had great curves and huge breasts and Cyl sucked one then the other as they stood under the water. She dropped to her knee and took Luna in her mouth.

"Oh, God," moaned Luna. "Oh dear God I'm going to come."

And come she did. All over Cyl's face. Cyl couldn't have been happier.

"You two almost through in there?" Martinique stood in the bathroom watching them through the door.

"Almost," said Luna.

They got out, dried, and dressed and headed into Ybor City for the supposed best steak in Tampa.

After dinner, they searched Cyl's MacBook for Jane Does in Havana. There wasn't any information on anything prior to the eighteen hundreds.

"You really think we'll find more information in Havana?" said Martinique.

"I think we will. There's bound to be a library around there. Not that we'll understand much since it won't be in English."

"Hablo Español," said Luna.

"Do you really?" Cyl was duly impressed.

"That's awesome," sad Martinique. "So you'll be in charge."

"Sound good to me. I'll explain to the librarian what we're looking for and see if she can help us."

"Excellent. Now that that's settled, we should go to bed," said Martinique.

"Didn't you get enough today?" Cyl laughed.

"Never. I will never ever have gotten enough."

"I love that about you," Cyl said.

"Me, too," said Luna.

They went to bed and made love until the early morning. Cyl was tired but happy when she finally fell asleep.

CHAPTER TWENTY-TWO

It was late Friday night when they landed in Havana. The air was just as heavy as in Tampa and Cyl couldn't wait to get to the hotel and air conditioning. She got them checked in to their suite and they enjoyed their Jacuzzi bath before crashing for the night.

Cyl woke before the others the next morning and took a cup of coffee out onto the balcony. It was already muggy and she almost regretted stepping outside. But the lush, tropical view made it almost worthwhile.

Besides, she didn't want to disturb the others. She had a lot on her mind, and it was nice to sit outside and reflect on things. Did she believe they'd find Aurnia? She didn't believe they had a snowball's chance in hell. But she would do everything in her power to find her. She couldn't handle seeing Luna so desolate again. And she hated disappointing Brigid.

She heard the others moving around so stepped inside.

"Y'all ready to get our day going?"

"Yep," said Martinique.

"Heck yeah," Luna said. "I'm ready to find Aurnia."

"Great. So when we get to the library, we need to ask the librarian where the oldest cemetery in the city is. Then we need to find out how old it is. I have a feeling that's where we'll find Aurnia."

"And I hope they have a record of who's buried where," said Martinique.

"I'm sure they will," said Cyl.

They arrived as the library opened and had the place to themselves that morning. They approached the librarian who seemed grateful that Luna spoke Spanish.

They conversed for quite a while and although Cyl had no clue what was being said, Luna seemed animated and excited. This seemed to be a good sign. She finally thanked the librarian and joined the others.

"What did we find out?" Cyl said.

"The oldest cemetery here is the Necrópolis Cristóbal Colón. But it was built in the late eighteen hundreds. Before then, people were buried in crypts at local churches. The oldest church in town is the Church of the Holy Spirit, which was a black church that was built in sixteen hundred and thirty-eight. So none of the old churches are still standing, but this library has books on unclaimed dead and where they might be buried."

"Let's find those books," said Cyl.

"Right this way." Luna had a spring in her step which had been missing since the failed boat attempt to find Aurnia. She swayed her hips in a way that made Cyl's palms itch to grab her and have her way with her.

Luna found the section she was looking for.

"Here we are," she said. "There are lots of volumes, so let's each take a section and start reading."

Cyl felt like they were trying to find a needle in a haystack, but had to do what she could to help. She was poring over entry after entry, skimming through the ones that couldn't possibly have been Aurnia.

"Here," said Martinique. "I have an entry of an unknown woman who washed ashore about a week after Aurnia died. She was found to have died from consumption."

"Oh, my God," Luna seemed to have forgotten she was in a library. "That's got to be her."

"Sure sounds like it," said Cyl. "Where is she buried?"

She entered the coordinates into her phone.

"Let's go get her," said Luna.

"What do we do if we find her?" Martinique asked in the taxi. "Like, we can't just dig her up and take her on the plane."

"You leave that to me," Cyl said. "I'll take care of the exhumation and relocation."

"You're so awesome," said Luna. "I love how you take care of things."

"That's my job." Cyl winked at her from the front seat.

The taxi stopped and the driver asked if they wanted him to wait.

"No, thanks," said Cyl. "We'll call for another cab when we're through here."

They trudged through the field which was overgrown with weeds. Cyl had downloaded a compass app on her phone to get the exact location. They found several dirt mounds throughout the field, and there was one all by itself at the coordinates.

"Oh, my God," Luna exclaimed. "We found her."

"Yes, we did." Cyl appreciated Luna's tight hug.

"Now to get her home," said Martinique.

"The embassy won't be open until Monday. I'll stay behind and make the arrangements. In the meantime, let's pull these weeds and make her space presentable."

They worked until they were tired, sore, and hungry. They headed back to the hotel where they each took a long, hot shower, then caught a cab for dinner.

Martinique and Luna enjoyed Mojitos while Cyl stuck to the trusty cuba libre. They finished their dinner and decided to find a club since they had no plans for Sunday except for Luna and Martinique flying home.

They found a women's club in a renovated cathedral. The high ceilings and stained glass windows appealed to Cyl. She liked the ambiance. She didn't like being reminded of all the times she'd been forced to go to Mass as a kid, but the music and women got her over that quickly.

They danced and drank and danced some more. They were just coming off the dance floor when Luna said, "I'm horny. Let's go back to the hotel."

"Nonsense," Martinique laughed. "There's a restroom. Surely you remember those days."

"Will you?" Luna looked to Cyl with pleading eyes.

"Why not?"

They made their way to the restroom and were all over each other when they finally got a stall. Cyl slid her hand under Luna's dress and found her center bare. No undies. What a turn-on. She drilled her deep and rubbed her clit until Luna bit her shoulder to keep from screaming.

"Your turn," Luna whispered.

"No way."

"Yes. Please?"

Luna unzipped Cyl's shorts and found Cyl's hotspot. She fingered it then pressed her fingers into Cyl's swollen clit until Cyl felt the world spin off its axis as she rode the waves of the orgasm.

"All better?" Martinique said when they arrived at the table.

"Oh, yeah," said Luna. "I'm good for a couple more hours anyway."

They all laughed and relaxed with their drinks. Cyl glanced at her watch. It was after three.

"We need to get you two home. You need some sleep before the plane."

"No," said Luna. "I'm having fun."

"As am I," said Martinique. "But Cyl is right. Come on, Miss Horny. Let's get back to the hotel."

"I'm going to relax in the tub." Luna stripped. "Anyone care to join me?"

"How is that sleeping?" Cyl laughed.

"You join me in this tub and I guarantee it'll help me sleep."

"Why not?" said Martinique.

Cyl watched her two women making out in the Jacuzzi. Hands were roaming, mouths were open, tongues obviously tangoing. She could go to bed and let them take care of each other, but they looked so fucking hot that her hormones surged. She stripped and joined them.

She sat across the tub from them, wondering if they'd even notice her. No biggie. She was enjoying watching. And the bubbles helped ease her sore muscles from pulling all those weeds.

Cyl watched and Luna arched her back, screamed, then settled back into place with a smile on her face. Mission accomplished, Martinique. Well done. Cyl grinned.

"I'm going to need both of you now," Martinique said. "Luna, you hold me up."

Martinique rested her legs on either side of Cyl, pressed her pussy into Cyl's face, while Luna supported her. Cyl grabbed Martinique's hips and held her close while she devoured every delicious inch.

"Oh, fuck," Martinique cried as she bounced her hips up and down on Cyl's face. "Oh holy fuck, I'm gonna come."

Her whole body tensed as she screamed then went limp. Luna eased her back to her feet and Cyl licked her lips. Yum.

They climbed into bed together, all snuggled into each other, and fell into a deep sleep.

Cyl woke around noon to an empty bed. She dressed quickly and stepped out onto the balcony where Martinique and Luna sat with their coffee.

"How long have you two been up?"

"About an hour," said Martinique. "We were going to wake you, but figured you could use your sleep."

"Appreciate that. Damn. I'm hungry. Y'all want breakfast?"

"Oh, my God," said Luna. "You just said 'Y'all.' I'm so proud of you."

Martinique laughed.

"She did, didn't she? That's awesome. We're rubbing off on you."

"I suppose you are. Now, breakfast?"

"Sure," said Martinique.

"If you're going to shower, do it fast, because I'm starving."

They all dressed and took a taxi to Old Town. They dined on huge servings and consumed massive amounts of coffee. Cyl was feeling much more human after they were finished.

They walked around for a while then it was time for Luna and Martinique to pack and get ready for their flight.

"I'm going to miss you two," Cyl said. "Take care of each other for me?"

"Of course," said Martinique.

"I'll probably be home tomorrow night."

"Sounds good," said Luna.

Cyl was at the embassy as soon as it opened. She wanted answers and was too excited to sleep in. She got there only to have to wait since she didn't have an appointment, but she didn't mind. It gave her time to rehearse yet again what she would say.

She was finally called in at ten. She took a deep breath and walked in like she knew what she was doing. Fake it til you make it was her motto. And she planned on getting what she wanted.

"Cyl Waterford?" the ambassador said. "How can I help you?"

"Short version is one of my relatives is buried here and I'd like to take her back to Tampa to be buried properly."

"A relative? What's her name?"

"Aurnia Gallagher."

"And how did she come to be buried here?"

"She washed ashore after being buried at sea." Cyl set her folder on his desk and showed him all the information she had.

"Oh, wow. You've certainly done your research. And what relation is this woman to you?"

Cyl got the family tree folder from her backpack and set it on his desk.

"She's my great-great-great-great-aunt or something like that. Here. See if you can figure it out."

She went on while he reviewed the tree.

"Her husband is buried on my property. I'd like her to join him. If that's not possible, I'd at least like her in a cemetery in Tampa."

"And where is she buried now?"

"In the middle of a field. I could take you there."

"Are you sure it's her?"

"I am."

"Exhumations are serious business," he said. "We don't do them lightly. Can you tell me what you mean by 'middle of a field'?"

"She was buried way back when. We found the coordinates in the library. We found her there. So there are no markers. It's not a cemetery. I doubt it was even consecrated ground."

"Well, that helps. I'll try to make this happen for you. I don't see why it won't. It's an unusual request to be sure, but I don't think anyone would mind."

"Thank you, sir."

"My pleasure. I have your information, so I'll call you when you can come pick her up."

"Thank you again. Have a great day."

Cyl walked out feeling like she was on top of the world. She couldn't wait to tell Luna and Martinique. She couldn't wait to get home to them.

She went to a nearby tavern and had lunch and a beer to kill time before she had to catch her flight.

The flight home was uneventful and Luna and Martinique were both at the airport to greet her. She hadn't realized how much she'd miss them. They had become such an integral part of her life. And she wouldn't trade that for anything.

Chapter Twenty-three

They had just finished dinner and Cyl had some news she was dreading delivering.

"We need to talk, y'all."

"I just love when you say 'y'all,'" said Luna.

"As do I. But you sound so serious," Martinique said.

"I have to fly back to Fort Collins for a few days."

"How long is a few days?" said Martinique.

"And will you really come back? Or is this a way to soften the blow?"

"I'll really come back," said Cyl. "I just got news that my office has been vandalized. Some friends boarded up the window, but I need to go back and deal with the police."

"Your office. In Fort Collins," said Martinique. "I forget that that's where you belong."

"Don't do that," said Cyl. "I belong here. With you two. And I know that now. I need to deal with the police and close my office there. I plan to open a new one here."

"For real?" said Luna.

"For real," said Cyl.

"So we can relax and be a throuple forever?" Martinique said.

"Yes. Forever."

"Woot!" Luna broke into a wide smile.

"I'm so happy to hear that," said Martinique. "So very. I've been loving this time, but waiting for the other shoe to drop."

"No other shoe. No dropping," said Cyl. "I'm staying here with you two."

"When are you going to Fort Collins?"

"Tomorrow. I'd love it if one of you could give me a ride to the airport on your way to work."

"I will," said Martinique.

"Thank you."

"And you swear you're coming back?" Luna said.

"I swear. I'll be gone a few days. But then I'll be flying home for good. Y'all could do me a favor while I'm gone."

"What's that?"

"Get rid of my aunt's stuff. Donate it to whoever you think she'd want. But I need a place for my clothes, etc. So please clean out the closet and anything I left in her dressers."

"That will be hard," said Luna.

"Yes, it will," said Martinique. "But if Cyl is going to move in properly, we need to do it."

"Thank you," said Cyl.

"We'll take care of it," Luna said. "Your aunt used to work with a women's shelter. I'll see if I can find any information on how to donate to them."

"That sounds perfect," said Cyl. "Now, what should we do with our evening?"

"Let's visit Brigid," said Luna. "It's been a few weeks. Maybe she's calmed down."

"Maybe," said Cyl. "And it's getting darker earlier so it won't be a middle of the night type of meeting. Let's have some drinks then go see her. She still doesn't know about Aurnia anyway."

"You think we should tell her?" Luna said. "What if it doesn't happen?"

"I think she deserves to know we've found her and are trying to bring her home."

"I agree," said Martinique.

After a couple of beers and glasses of wine it was dark enough to go summon Brigid. Brigid arrived promptly and announced her presence by knocking on the table.

"We have news," said Cyl. "We found Aurnia."

"Yes," Martinique said. "It turns out she'd washed ashore and is buried in Havana. We've seen her grave."

"Cyl has petitioned to bring her home," said Luna. "Isn't this exciting?" One knock.

The pen hovered.

Thank you.

"You're quite welcome. I met with the ambassador and he's going to work on us bringing her back here. He said it shouldn't be a problem at all." One knock.

"Do you have any questions for us?" said Luna.

My treasure?

"What about it?" Cyl said. "Should we bury it here?" Two knocks.

Yours now.

"That's what you said, but I don't know about that, Brigid," said Martinique. "It's rightfully yours." Two knocks.

I'm dead.

"True," Cyl said. "But what will we do with it?"

Rich.

"We would be," said Luna. "But we don't want to go against your wishes."

Yours.

"Okay," said Cyl. "Do you insist?" One knock.

"I'm not entirely sure what we'll do with it," Martinique said. "We may have to donate it to a museum or something." Two knocks.

Yours.

"Right," said Cyl. "We'll figure it out."

"So, we're okay now?" said Luna. One knock. "Excellent."

"I hate to break up the party," said Cyl. "But I've got an early flight and these two have to work tomorrow. Take care, Brigid, and we'll be back." One knock.

When the room had warmed to a normal temperature, they switched on the lights then headed back to the cottage.

"Seriously," said Martinique. "What are we going to do with all that treasure?"

"Somehow we have to get it appraised, but who would appraise four-hundred-year-old coins and jewels?" Luna said.

"We'll figure it all out," said Cyl. "Jewelers should be able to appraise the jewels, even jewels that old. The coins? That's going to be trickier."

"And all the gold..." Martinique said.

"We'll get it appraised. We don't need to appraise it all at once. There's enough there for our descendants to live comfortably."

"You're right," said Luna.

"Good point," Martinique said.

"I'm turning in. Anybody want to join me?"

"I suppose we should. Tomorrow's Monday. Ugh," said Martinique.

Cyl woke early and showered before Martinique and Luna were up. She didn't want to interfere with their morning routines. She was dressed, packed, and sipping coffee before the other two ever woke.

They came into the kitchen, each of them naked as the day they were born. And looking all adorable with morning faces. Cyl fought the urge to take them back to bed and mess around for a little bit. She didn't have that kind of time. And they certainly didn't. What a shame.

"Good morning, sleeping beauties. How are y'all doing?"

"Coffee," mumbled Martinique.

Cyl laughed.

"You two fill your mugs and I'll make another pot."

When it was time to leave, Luna hugged Cyl tight.

"You promise you're coming back?"

"Scout's honor. I'll be back before you know it."

"No, that's not possible," said Martinique. "Now, come on. Let's get you dropped off."

"Safe travels," said Luna. "And keep in touch while you're out there."

"Y'all will get tired of hearing from me."

"Never." Luna planted a powerful kiss on Cyl's mouth and Cyl had to take a moment to regain her balance.

At the airport, Martinique hugged Cyl.

"No kiss from me. I'm not into public displays of affection."
Cyl grinned.

"Understood. I'll be back soon."

"Good-bye, Cyl."

"Take care, Martinique."

It was early when she landed in Fort Collins, and she went straight to the police station.

"May I help you?" A gruff older gentleman sat behind the desk.

"Cyl Waterford to meet with Detective Martinelli."

He gave her a once-over then picked up the phone.

"There's a Cyl Waterford here to see you, ma'am."

He hung up the phone and pointed to a metal chair.

"Have a seat. She'll be with you when she can."

That sounded promising. Not. Cyl sat and tried to get comfortable as she settled in to wait until Detective Martinelli might have time for her. She was lost in social media land when she heard a rich voice.

"Ms. Waterford?"

She looked up to see a tall, muscular woman who looked to be in her early forties. Still, she was stunning.

"Yes." Cyl stood and offered her hand. "Detective Martinelli?"

"That's me. Let's head over to your office and get the inventory done."

"Sounds good."

Cyl went through everything that was missing. They had gotten two laptops and some pencils. They'd trashed the place though, probably looking for more portable objects to steal.

"We didn't see a safe here," Martinelli said.

"No. No need for one of those. I really don't think they got much. Maybe a hundred dollars' worth of mechanical pencils and ten thousand worth of laptops. They were MacBooks after all."

"Okay. Do you have the serial numbers for the Macs?"

"At my condo. That's where I dealt with the business end of things. This office was just for meeting clients and having a face in the community. I'd come here and draft, but paperwork and stuff were kept in my home office."

"I guess that's where we're heading now," said Martinelli.

"Yeah. Can I call someone to replace the window first?"

"Not yet. Sorry."

"Shit."

"I understand. We'll be through here in a couple of hours."

"Thanks," said Cyl.

She found the serial numbers of the MacBooks and gave them to Martinelli. She found the most recent receipt for purchasing the pencils and gave it to the detective as well.

"Not that I care about those. I mean, it pisses me off, but they're not that big of a deal. They're replaceable."

"I think I have all I need from you," Martinelli said. "I'll give you a lift back to the station."

"Appreciate that. But I've got my truck. I can get from place to place with it."

"That's right. So you live here but were on vacation when this happened?"

"Yes and no. I inherited some property in Tampa and was planning on selling it, but things have happened and it looks like I'm relocating there permanently."

"I've never been to Florida. Is it beautiful?"

"In a different way, yes. I miss the mountains and the cool, dry air. Tampa is flat and hot and muggy as hell. But the palm trees are nice and the gulf is gorgeous."

Martinelli laughed.

"Don't work for the chamber of commerce there, okay?"

"No worries there."

"Thanks for all your help. I'll text you when you can get the window repaired."

"Thank you."

Cyl walked Martinelli to the door then looked around her condo. When had she accumulated so much shit? She'd have to decide what to sell and what to ship. She spent the rest of the morning making lists and arranging shipping. She called a friend who graciously agreed to sell what Cyl was leaving behind for her.

She got the text that she was good to repair the window so went to the office to supervise. While there, Cyl called the city and canceled her business license. When everything was taken care of, she called Luna.

"Cyl! How are you?"

"I'm great. How are you? How's Martinique?"

"We're boring. We need you here with us. When are you flying home?"

"Change of plans. I'm driving."

"You're what?"

Cyl laughed.

"It will take a few extra days, but I want my truck with me in Tampa."

"Can't you sell it and buy a new one here?" Luna sounded desperate.

"Negative. Look, I'm heading out now. I'll go as far as I can tonight."

"Please be careful."

"I will. Can I talk to Martinique now?"

Martinique came on the line.

"What in the hell are you thinking?" she said.

"I'm thinking I'll be home in a few days. Will you two survive without me?"

"Barely."

Cyl laughed again.

"I'm sure you'll find something to do to keep you entertained."

"No doubt there. But it's still not the same without you here."

"I'll be home soon," Cyl reiterated. "Hold down the fort for me, okay?"

"You got it, stud."

"I miss you two."

"We miss you too."

"Okay, well if I want to get a head start on this road trip, I'd better get a move on. I'll see y'all soon."

"Take care and drive carefully."

Cyl wasn't used to missing people but she missed Luna and Martinique more than she ever thought possible. She would drive carefully. Fast, but carefully. She needed to get home.

CHAPTER TWENTY-FOUR

Things settled back to normal once Cyl was home again. Things seemed more relaxed with Martinique and Luna as more and more packages of Cyl's belongings showed up at the cottage. They seemed to believe Cyl was there to stay and that made them happier and hornier than before. If that was possible.

Cyl had gotten permits to add a bathroom onto the cottage off the guest bedroom. She wanted a functioning bathroom for when she tore apart the master and put in a shower they could all fit in and a Jacuzzi tub. So she spent her days adding on the new bathroom and her nights making love with Martinique and Luna. Life was good. Really good. Better than she'd ever dreamed it could be.

When she had the cottage set up as she wanted it, she planned to look for an office in Ybor City and get back to work. This long, unintended sabbatical had been nice, but it was time to get back to doing what she did best.

One morning, as she was finishing up the spare bathroom, her phone rang.

"Hello?"

"Cyl? This is the ambassador to Cuba. We met about six weeks ago?"

"Yes, sir. Thank you for calling. Is this good news? Or bad news?"

"It's very good news. You've received permission to take Aurnia Gallagher home."

"Outstanding! Thank you so much. When can I come get her?"

"You let me know. I'll arrange the exhumation. You'll probably want to purchase a casket. Chances are she was just thrown into the grave."

"I understand. I can be there next week."

"Excellent."

They ironed out the details and Cyl hung up jubilant. She wanted to shout from the highest mountain, not that there were any in Tampa. She texted Luna and Martinique and went back to work while she waited for their replies.

Neither had texted back within an hour and it was four o'clock so she called it a day. She looked up funeral homes in Havana and started checking out caskets. She realized she was getting ahead of herself. She needed a place to bury Aurnia.

She called the city and inquired about burying Aurnia on her property next to her husband, but the city refused to permit it. No matter how much Cyl tried to persuade and cajole, the city wouldn't budge. So this meant she needed to bury her somewhere in Tampa. She decided to wait until the other two got home to make any decisions.

Cyl had just popped the top on a cold one when she heard tires on her driveway. Someone was home. Luna came in and hugged Cyl tight.

"I got your text," she said. "But I was in a meeting. That's so fantastic that we get to bring Aurnia home."

"I know. I'm so excited."

Martinique came in and found them in an embrace.

"Group hug?" she said.

They moved apart and welcomed her in.

"Isn't it fantastic?" said Luna.

"What?"

"Did you not get my text?"

"No," said Martinique. "What's up?"

"I'm flying to Havana next week to bring Aurnia home."

"Oh, my God. That's fantastic. Will we bury her here? On the point?"

"No can do," said Cyl. "So we need to decide where to bury her and what casket to bury her in. I've got the sites bookmarked. Let's take a look."

"I think we should bury her in Ybor City," said Martinique. "I think it would be fitting."

"The gayborhood? That makes sense," said Cyl.

She pulled it up on the Mac and only found an Italian and a Spanish cemetery.

"So it doesn't look like that will work," said Luna. "That's too bad. Let's keep looking."

"Oaklawn is very historic," said Martinique. "But I don't know if it's open for new burials."

"Let's find out," said Cyl.

They agreed on the cemetery. Oaklawn it was. It would be pricey but if they all pitched in, they could cover it.

"You're very expensive, stud," said Luna. "I've spent more money since being involved with you."

Cyl laughed.

"I wasn't the one who wanted to summon a ghost, which is what started all of this, if you recall."

"True. Very true," said Luna.

"Now we need to decide on a casket. I've found some funeral homes in Havana. We just need to decide on which one and then choose the casket."

They spent the next half hour perusing caskets and finally all agreed on a solid mahogany casket with a velvet interior. With everything decided, Cyl closed her laptop.

"Now what?" she said.

"Let's celebrate!" said Luna.

"Want me to go pick up some bubbly?" said Cyl.

"No. I want you in the bedroom. Now."

"Oh yeah. Now you're talking," said Martinique.

Luna and Cyl were in a hot and heavy make out session while Martinique sucked Cyl's nipples and fingered Luna. Soon Luna forgot about kissing Cyl so Cyl took Martinique in her mouth.

She savored the flavor that was Martinique's alone as she swirled her tongue over every inch of her. Inside and out Cyl used her tongue to elicit moans of delight from Martinique. She heard Luna cry out her release and that spurned her onward.

Her own crotch was spasming with need, but she was determined to get Martinique off first. She replaced her mouth with her fingers and sucked Martinique's small, firm breasts. Soon Martinique called out Cyl's name as she rode the orgasm Cyl had provided.

Cyl was hornier than she could ever remember being. These two women took her places she'd only dreamed of. And she couldn't wait to feel them take her there again.

Luna ran her fingers between Cyl's legs.

"Someone's wet," she cried.

"Imagine that."

"I mean, holy shit, you are wet."

"Are you going to do something about that?" said Cyl.

"I'm going to eat you till you scream."

"Oh God, that sounds good."

Luna lowered her mouth and sucked Cyl's lower lips. She ran her tongue between them then sucked again. The sensation was incredible. Martinique was back suckling Cyl's nipple and the combination of their actions had Cyl teetering. Was it too soon? Did they care if she couldn't hold out?

She lost her ability to think when Luna's talented tongue found her clit. She flicked it, sucked it, and lapped at it and soon Cyl left her body as the force of the climax hit.

"I'm hungry now," said Martinique.

"I'm still horny," said Luna.

"You're always horny." Cyl laughed.

"That's because I'm in a relationship with the two sexiest women alive."

"Aw. Thank you. For that, I'll give you one more orgasm before we have dinner."

Cyl lay back and watched Martinique please Luna. Her face was buried between Luna's legs and Luna's hand was on the back of Martinique's head. Cyl knew how good Luna must feel and absently began stroking herself as she watched.

Martinique took Luna to another orgasm and then glanced at Cyl.

"Holy shit. That's a hot sight," she said. "I'm going to join you."

And while Luna recovered from her second coming, Cyl and Martinique got themselves off for each other's entertainment. It had been a great evening.

"Now let's have dinner."

"I don't want to get dressed to cook," said Luna. "Let's order in."

They placed their order.

"Since we're lying around naked, who's going to get the food?" said Cyl.

"Whoever can go the longest without coming," Martinique said.

"What?"

"We're going to masturbate mutually again. And whoever holds out the longest has to get the food. They're welcome to do it naked or dressed, but they have to get it."

"Oh, shit," said Luna. "I like the way you think."

They all propped themselves up on the headboard and when Martinique gave the orders, they began pleasuring themselves. Cyl knew she was going to lose, but didn't care. She was certain she was the hardest one to get off.

But the sights and sounds of her lovers fingering themselves proved to be a wonderful libido jump start. Soon the scent of women loving themselves filled the air and Cyl actually cried out first.

She so wanted to help the other two reach their climaxes, but rules were rules. She sat back and enjoyed the show. Luna cried out once and then again before Martinique finally reached her pinnacle of pleasure.

"Shit. I'll get dressed," Martinique said.

She pulled on one of Cyl's old T-shirts and went to the door. It barely covered her goodies and Cyl hoped she didn't give the driver a show. But, knowing Martinique, she hoped she would.

They sat at the table and ate then Cyl had a thought.

"Let's go see Brigid. She needs to know we're bringing Aurnia home."

"Good idea," said Luna.

They got dressed and went to the lighthouse. They summoned Brigid for over an hour before she finally knocked on the table.

"We have news for you," said Luna.

"I'm bringing Aurnia back to Tampa next week," Cyl said. One knock.

"We can't bury her here," said Martinique. "But she'll be in a cemetery here in town so you'll be able to visit her." One knock.

"We wanted to tell you. We'll give you all the details of her plot location once she's buried," said Luna. One knock.

"That's all we wanted to tell you. We'll reach out again if we have any more updates," Cyl said.

The pen hovered.

Thank you.

"You're so very welcome. See you later, Brigid," said Luna. One knock.

Back at the cottage, Luna seemed down for some reason.

"You okay?" Cyl said.

"Just bummed you'll be leaving again."

"Y'all can come with."

"It's too short notice for me to get time off," Martinique said.

"You could call in sick."

"No. You can do this. And Luna can go with you if she wants."

"I think I'd like that," said Luna. "How long do you think we'll be gone?"

"Just overnight. But I'd like both of you to be at the cemetery when she's laid to rest."

"Of course," said Martinique. "We'll figure out all the details tomorrow and then we can make our plans."

"I'm excited now," said Luna. "We're going on another adventure. And this time we know we're bringing her home."

"Exactly."

The next day Cyl got everything situated. She called the funeral home in Havana and got the casket. She called the ambassador and left the message that she'd be there Wednesday evening and wanted to take Aurnia home Thursday. She booked flights for herself and Luna. She was ready.

She got a call back from the ambassador. They would exhume Aurnia Thursday morning at daybreak. The hearse would transport her to the airport.

"That sounds great," said Cyl. "So we should be able to fly out early Thursday morning?"

"That's correct. I'll accompany you so there are no unforeseen issues."

"Thank you so much. I appreciate this."

"You'll need a hearse standing by at the airport in Tampa to transport her. Have you set that up?"

"No, sir. I'll make that call right now."

"Sounds good. I'll see you Thursday."

"Good-bye."

Cyl called the airline and switched their flight to earlier in the morning. Then she called Oaklawn to let them know her plans. With all that set, she called a local funeral home and ordered a hearse to bring Aurnia to the cemetery.

Everything was in place. She was set. They were set. What an adventure it had been. What a crazy fucking adventure since the moment she'd heard she'd inherited this from Aunt Marjorie.

She'd never imagined she'd be living in Tampa flippin' Florida. And hadn't ever dreamed of searching for, let alone recovering, sunken treasure. She never, ever thought she'd commune with a ghost. Hell, she hadn't even believed in them.

And she'd never pictured herself in a relationship, let alone a throuple. Life was weird. It was very weird and filled with unexpected twists and turns, but she wouldn't trade her life for anything. She was happy. Happier than she ever thought possible.

Chapter Twenty-Five

The plane touched down in Tampa just past noon. Cyl and Luna waited until everyone had disembarked then got off and found the hearse and limo waiting to take them to Oaklawn.

They watched as Aurnia was carefully removed from the plane and placed in the hearse. Cyl still couldn't believe this was happening. Aurnia was home. Or as close to home as they could get her.

When the chauffer opened the limo door, Martinique was waiting for them, looking absolutely devourable in a little black dress. She was stunning and as Cyl kissed her hello, she almost forgot the reason for Martinique's attire.

"I'm glad everything went smoothly," said Martinique.

"Me, too. One last stop for Aurnia."

"Indeed," said Luna.

"I did something yesterday I think you'll be interested in."

"Yeah?" said Cyl. "What's that?"

"I took a strand of pearls to the jeweler."

"You did?" Luna said. "Good for you. What did you find out?"

"I got us ten thousand dollars. Not bad, huh?"

"Excellent," said Cyl. "That covers a lot. So what we'll do is take bits and pieces of the treasure to sell over time."

"That's what I was thinking," Martinique said.

"You two are geniuses," said Luna.

Cyl had her arm draped over Martinique's shoulders and was massaging Luna's shoulder with her hand. How had she lucked out?

She had found not one, but two beautiful women to spend her time with. The fates had smiled on her for sure. Maybe Aunt Marjorie was somewhere calling the shots. Who knew?

The ceremony was short and sweet. They watched as Aurnia was lowered into the ground at her final resting place. Feeling good that she'd managed to get Aurnia home, Cyl placed her arms around her two women and walked back to the limousine which took them back to the mortuary.

"Do you need to get back to the office?" Cyl said. "Or can you give us a lift home?"

"I took the afternoon off, so I'm all yours."

"I do like the sound of that."

Back at the cottage, they changed into more comfortable clothes and Cyl made them sandwiches for lunch.

"What shall we do with the rest of our day?" said Luna.

"I don't know," said Cyl. "I'm pretty wiped out from the enormity of what we did today."

"Yeah. I'm emotionally drained," said Martinique.

"So I guess we'll just watch TV and hang out?" Luna said.

"That sounds good to me," said Cyl.

They cleaned up their lunch dishes then settled on the couch and settled in to watch a lesbian romantic comedy. Cyl dozed off after the first few minutes and woke at the ending credits to find Luna and Martinique snoring softly. She supposed they were all wiped out.

She left them sleeping on the couch and took a couple of beers and headed for the point. She sat in the grass and watched the gulf. It was peaceful. She opened a beer and took a swig. She was where she needed to be. No doubt. She loved sitting on the point and staring at the water. It was so peaceful, so reassuring somehow.

Cyl was about to open her second beer when she heard voices. She turned to see Luna and Martinique approaching with a bottle of wine and two glasses.

"Fancy meeting you here," Cyl said.

"We worried when we woke up and you were gone," said Luna.

"But we checked the lighthouse and saw you out here. Hope you don't mind that we opted to join you," Martinique said.

"Mind? Hell, no. I'm happy you did."

Cyl opened their wine and poured them each a glass.

"We need to set up a picnic table or something out here," she said.

"That would be nice," said Luna.

"Yeah. I think I'll get one. It's hard for y'all to balance your wine glasses on the grass."

"But it's so nice sitting here on the grass with you two," Martinique said.

"Well, that's true."

They sat in silence for a while, each lost in their own thoughts. Martinique stood which brought Cyl back to the moment.

"What are you doing?" She looked up and saw Martinique stripping.

"I need you. Now."

"I like the way you think." Luna also stood and removed her clothes.

The sight of the two naked beauties lying next to her almost made Cyl forget where they were. Almost.

"I'll gladly take care of you two, but no way I'm getting naked out here in broad daylight."

"Fair enough," said Martinique. "I can please you with your clothes on."

"I'm well aware," said Cyl. And she was grateful for that. She was a swollen, wet mess and knew she'd be desperate for release after taking care of her lovers.

Two naked beauties lying beside her and Cyl didn't even know where to begin. She kissed Martinique hard on her mouth then kissed Luna the same way. Each of them kissed her back showing their need.

Cyl took one of Luna's large breasts in her mouth while Luna and Martinique kissed each other open-mouthed. Cyl sucked and tugged until Luna's nipple could have cut glass. She dragged her hand between Martinique's legs and found her wet and ready for her. She plunged her fingers deep while sucking Luna's other tit. She was becoming more aroused by the moment and thought she might self-combust.

She continued to move in and out of Martinique as she kissed lower and lower on Luna until she was between her legs. She took Luna in her mouth and had to really focus on her fingers inside Martinique. Luna tasted so fucking good and felt so slick on her tongue. She wanted to bury her fingers inside Luna while she sucked her clit, but knew Martinique needed attention as well.

Cyl dragged her fingers across Martinique's swollen clit and Martinique bucked her hips and moaned loudly. Cyl glanced up then and saw the others had quit making out. Each lay there with their eyes closed lost in the feelings Cyl was creating.

She pressed her fingers into Martinique's clit while she sucked and tongued Luna's. They cried out at the same time. They were loud, long screams that pierced the afternoon quiet.

Cyl's nipples ached and the throbbing between her legs made her desperate for attention. But Luna and Martinique just lay there catching their breath.

"I need you," Martinique finally said. "I need taste you. Take off your shorts."

Cyl was so horny, she was half tempted to oblige.

"No can do," she said.

"Fine," said Martinique who unbuttoned Cyl's shorts and pulled them down around her ankles. "Now I can get you."

She buried her face between Cyl's legs. Cyl lay back and Luna pulled Cyl's shirt up and sucked her nipples. Damn, they felt good. They each had tongues that could work magic and it didn't take long for Cyl to close her eyes and watch the light show unfold as she came hard and fast.

She opened her eyes to find Luna and Martinique had apparently forgotten about her. Luna was on the ground with Martinique on top of her, her pussy in Luna's mouth. Cyl sat up and watched Luna and Martinique eat each other into oblivion. Damn. That was hot.

Cyl was ready for another turn, but again she had to wait. Martinique finally rolled off Luna and kissed Cyl hard on her mouth.

The essence of Luna on her tongue did little to quell her raging hormones.

Luna rolled over then and slid her fingers deep inside Cyl. Oh, fuck yeah.

"That feels so fucking good," Cyl muttered. "Fuck me harder, Luna. Give it to me rough."

Luna did just that. There was no pretense of tenderness and she nailed Cyl. She used another finger and then another. Soon Cyl lost the ability to think as Luna pummeled her and Martinique sucked her.

The women sent Cyl soaring out of her body and into orbit. She floated back to her body and Luna was licking and sucking her pussy. She was being gentle and tender and it sent Cyl back into orbit in no time.

The three of them lay snuggled together for a while after.

"We should head back to the cottage," said Cyl. "Don't you think?"

"Only if you promise to get naked in bed with us," Martinique said.

"That's a promise I can definitely make," said Cyl.

Once back at the cottage, they removed each other's clothes then Luna went to the dresser and handed Cyl her strap-on. Cyl put it on while Luna got on all fours. Before Cyl could use the toy, Martinique went down on it and deep throated the dildo. She licked and sucked all over it until Cyl thought she'd explode from watching her.

Martinique finally finished and Cyl buried her cock inside Luna.

"Oh, yeah," said Luna. "Fuck me harder."

Cyl was happy to oblige. She moved her toy in and out of Luna, burying it deeper with each thrust. Martinique apparently didn't want to be left out as she slid under Luna and sucked one of her massive tits.

Cyl reached around Luna and rubbed her clit as she continued to fuck her and Luna screamed and collapsed on top of Martinique. Martinique managed to get out from under Luna and removed the dildo from its harness.

"On your back," she said to Cyl.

Cyl lay back and spread her legs. Martinique buried the dildo as far as she could then wrapped her lips around Cyl's clit. She sucked and fucked her until Cyl cried out and came harder than she could ever remember coming before.

She opened her eyes and saw Luna between Martinique's legs, feasting. The sight and sounds were so hot that Cyl couldn't resist touching herself. She stroked her clit while watching Luna finish off Martinique.

Luna moved over and pushed Cyl's fingers out of the way and took her in her mouth. Her talented tongue proved no match for Cyl whose whole body tensed then white heat flooded her as she rode her orgasm.

They lay together, limbs entwined when Cyl heard noises outside.

"Did y'all hear that?" she said.

"Mm," Martinique said drowsily. "Probably just Brigid."

"I'm going to check it out."

"No," said Luna. "I'm sure Martinique is right. Don't get dressed."

"I need to."

Cyl pulled on her shorts and shirt then stepped out the front door. There were three people at the lighthouse, one with strawberry blond hair.

"Tawny?" Cyl called.

Tawny turned and looked at her as the other two ran off.

"Get back here!" Cyl called after the others, but they were well down the road where they got into a car and drove off.

"Looks like it's just you," Cyl said to Tawny.

"Whatever. Give me what is mine and you'll never see me again."

"We don't have a damned thing that belongs to you. Now get off my property before I call the cops."

"You do and I'll tell them all about your treasure."

"What the fuck is wrong with you, Tawny? When did you turn into such a greedy bitch?"

"Greedy? Me? Look in the mirror," said Tawny.

"Get out of here. Get out and don't come back."

"Oh, I'll be back. You can count on it." She ran off toward the neighborhood. Cyl didn't have it in her to follow.

"Shit," she said.

She walked over to the lighthouse door which had been partially pried open. They were obviously after the treasure chest and Cyl was fuming. She went back inside.

"Tawny and some friends were trying to get into the lighthouse," Cyl said. "Come on, you two. It's time to move the treasure chest inside the cottage."

"No shit?" Luna was up and getting dressed.

"No shit. Come on, Martinique. We need all three of us to move it."

They got the treasure chest under the dining room table. It took a lot of maneuvering and resting, but they got it done.

"Tawny's got a lot of nerve," Cyl said.

"I can't believe she tried to break into the lighthouse," said Luna.

"I need to go fix the door."

"Can we help?" Martinique said.

"No. You two stay here. I'll be right back."

Cyl got the door fixed and went back to the cottage to find Martinique had made dinner.

"Come on in before it gets cold," she said.

They ate dinner then took showers then decided it was time to visit with Brigid. They needed to let her know Aurnia was home.

"Do you think Brigid will stay here now that Aurnia's in Tampa?" said Martinique.

"I doubt it," said Luna. "She'll probably relocate to Oaklawn."

"That's too bad," said Cyl. "I'll miss her."

"Won't we all?"

CHAPTER TWENTY-SIX

Brigid arrived after an hour of calling her. She knocked on the table to signify her presence just as Cyl was about to give up.

"We brought Aurnia home," Cyl said. "She's at Oaklawn Cemetery."

No response. Cyl gave her the plot number and still Brigid did nothing.

"Are you still here?" said Luna. One knock.

"Are you happy she's home?" Martinique said. One knock.

"Will you go see her?" said Cyl. One knock.

"Will you still live here?" Luna said. Two knocks.

"We'll miss you." Cyl couldn't believe she'd miss a ghost, but the truth was, she'd come to enjoy their visits with Brigid.

"Do you think Aurnia has a ghost?" Luna said. No response. Then the pen hovered.

Hope so.

"We hope so, too," said Martinique. "We like the idea of the two of you being together forever."

Thank you.

"You're welcome," said Cyl.

For everything.

"You're so very welcome," said Luna. "Enjoy the rest of your existence."

With Aurnia.

"Yes," said Cyl. "With Aurnia. Forever."

Good-bye.

"Good-bye, Brigid," Martinique said. "Take care."

The temperature went up and they turned on the lights. Cyl felt a sadness wash over her knowing Brigid was out of her life for good.

"She's gone and I never did do my story of the haunted lighthouse," said Luna.

"Well, now you can do the haunted cemetery. Film Oaklawn at night. I'm sure Brigid would make herself known for you," said Cyl.

"True. I think I'll do that."

"Great. Maybe you can meet Aurnia, too," Martinique said. "Wouldn't that be cool?"

"It would indeed," said Cyl.

"So what now?" said Luna. "Brigid is gone. The treasure is safe in the cottage. What do we do with ourselves now?"

"I don't know about you two, but I've got a cottage to renovate."

"Oh, I know what we'll do with our days, but our evenings and nights? What will we do for excitement?"

"Make love," said Martinique. "All night every night."

"I'm up for that," said Cyl.

"Me too." Luna laughed.

"Not tonight though," Cyl said. "I've given you enough for the day and you both need to work tomorrow."

"Ugh. Don't remind me," said Martinique.

"I'm going to get set up to film at Oaklawn," said Luna. "It's gonna be epic."

"Okay, well sleep first," said Cyl. "Come on, you two."

"Let's go up to the gallery first," said Martinique. "I want to gaze out at the gulf for a while."

"That sounds nice," said Luna.

"Works for me," Cyl said.

She picked up her beer and the wine bottle and led the way up to the top of the lighthouse. The lights of the city were visible, but when she turned off the lighthouse light, they could see the gulf stretched out before them.

"There's something so peaceful about sitting up here," said Cyl.

"And arousing," said Luna.

"What?"

"It's so still and quiet and we're all so close together away from everyone else. It's the perfect time to make love."

She stood and got undressed. Martinique joined her.

"You two," said Cyl. "You're insatiable exhibitionists."

"What's exhibitionist about wanting sex up here? The light's off. No one can see in," Martinique said. "Now, are you joining us?"

Without waiting for an answer, Martinique and Luna started making out. They were moaning into each other's mouths as their hands roamed.

"I may just watch the show this time," said Cyl.

"At least do it naked," Luna murmured.

Cyl stripped and sat back in her Adirondack and watched as Luna and Martinique pulled each other to the floor. They lay pressed together, nipple to nipple as their fingers searched between each other's legs.

It was soon too much for Cyl who set her beer down and eased herself onto the floor. Who gave a fuck if anyone could see them? Let them enjoy the show.

She took Luna's fingers out of Martinique and sucked them clean. Then she licked every last drop of Martinique's arousal, only to produce more. Martinique had the best flavor and Cyl couldn't get enough of her.

Martinique soon quit fucking Luna as Cyl eased her closer and closer to the edge. Far from being upset, Luna simply stroked herself as she watched Cyl eat Martinique. Martinique and Luna cried out together then turned their attention to Cyl who was wet and throbbing.

Martinique sucked Cyl's nipples while Luna fingered her into oblivion. When all three had climaxed, Cyl spoke.

"You two really need to get some sleep or you're going to be useless tomorrow."

"Mm. Let's sleep here," said Martinique.

"Let's not. Come on."

Cyl helped them up and they dressed in silence. Once back to the cottage, they all fell into bed exhausted.

Cyl woke the next morning alone. It was after nine so obviously the other two were at work. She finished the spare bathroom and went to work on remodeling the master bath. She was a jill of all trades and was fortunate not to have to hire anybody to help.

Her phone rang with a Fort Collins number so she answered it. "Hello?"

"Is this Ms. Waterford?"

"It is."

"This is Derek Prentiss with Fort Collins Realty?"

"Right. How can I help?" said Cyl.

"I'm calling to let you know we have an offer on your condo."

"Is that right? That's great."

Derek told her the offer and explained the buyer's terms. Cyl was in complete agreement with everything.

"How soon do they want to take ownership?"

"Well, once we let them know they can have it, we'll have a few weeks. We'll need you to come out and empty it, of course."

"Of course," said Cyl. "I'll fly out next weekend."

"Fantastic."

"I'll let you know the details after I've got everything arranged."

"Sounds good. Thank you, Ms. Waterford."

"Thank you."

When Martinique and Luna got home from work that evening, Cyl told them about her call from Derek.

"So I'll be flying to Fort Collins next weekend to put my things in storage for now," she said.

"Can we go?" Luna said.

"Would you like to?"

"Yeah," said Martinique. "I'd like to see your old stomping grounds."

"Great. We'll make a weekend out of it. We'll fly out after work Friday and come home Sunday night," said Cyl. "It'll be great."

"Excellent. Will you take us to a women's club while we're there? So we can see where you used to lure your victims?"

Cyl laughed. "Of course I will."

"This is gonna be great," said Luna. "I can't wait."

They landed in Denver at six thirty and rented a car to drive to Fort Collins. Cyl felt a certain pride as she drove them through town, showing them where her office used to be as well as her favorite haunts.

They arrived at her condo around eight thirty and though it was early, they were on East Coast time so crashed hard.

Cyl woke the next morning to Luna and Martinique exploring each other's bodies. Those two. They couldn't get enough of each other. Which was fair, since Cyl couldn't get enough of them either.

"What am I? Chopped liver?" she said.

"We didn't want to wake you," said Luna.

"I appreciate that. But I'm awake now."

The three of them made love until Martinique claimed she had no more in her. They showered, dressed, and walked down the street to get some breakfast. After breakfast, it was time to get to work.

They bought boxes and hired a moving van to take everything to storage. The place was empty by seven that evening. They returned the van and Cyl called Derek.

"The condo is empty," she said. "I'll meet you here tomorrow at say ten to give you my keys?"

"Sounds great. I'll be there. Thank you for getting it done so quickly."

"My pleasure," said Cyl. "I'm happy to make this happen."

"Okay. I'll see you in the morning."

They checked into a hotel for the night. They showered, dressed, then headed for Old Town to get dinner and go dancing. One of Cyl's favorite women's clubs was there and she was excited to share it with her women.

They followed the sound of the music after dinner and came to Muffs. Cyl paid everyone's cover and they went into an absolutely packed club. There was barely room to move, but Cyl fought her way to the bar to buy a bottle of champagne.

There were no tables available so they stood by the stage and sipped their champagne while they watched the DJ create her magic. EDM wasn't Cyl's type of music, but the beat was strong and eventually she convinced the others to hit the dance floor.

They danced and drank the night away. Cyl couldn't believe when last call came, but rather than buy another bottle, they decided to head out and beat the crowds.

"What did you think?" Cyl said.

"That was awesome. So much fun," said Luna.

"That really was a treat. Thanks, stud," Martinique said.

"I'm glad y'all enjoyed it. Now, I'm ready to crash."

"What time are you meeting the Realtor?" said Martinique.

"Ugh. Ten. I hope I make it."

"You will."

They fell into bed and Cyl closed her eyes and was out in an instant. She slept hard through the night, but then had strange, erotic dreams. She was dreaming she was at Muffs and everyone on the dance floor was naked. Then it turned into a giant orgy. Fingers and tongues were all over everywhere. She'd been pleasing a faceless woman when she felt a tongue on her. She awoke with a start to find Martinique between her legs.

"Good morning to me," she said.

"Couldn't have you miss your meeting," said Luna.

"Mm." said Martinique.

"What are you doing, Luna?" said Cyl. "You're not participating?"

"I'm watching."

It was then Cyl realized Luna was stroking herself while she kept her focus on Martinique. Damn that was hot.

"Get over here," Cyl said.

Luna moved over to Cyl, and they kissed briefly before Cyl slid her fingers inside Luna's hot tight center.

"Oh, fuck. That feels good," said Luna.

Cyl tried to focus on pleasing Luna, but Martinique had her brain turning to mush. She gave up on Luna and screamed as she rode the climax that Martinique had given her. She settled back to reality to find Martinique's mouth on Luna and heard Luna cry out.

"Your turn now," Cyl said to Martinique who climbed up and got comfortable on Cyl's face. Cyl licked and sucked and just basically devoured Martinique until she groaned and collapsed on Cyl.

"You've got to get going," said Luna. "Can't be late to the Realtor."

"Oh, shit. That's right. Okay. I'll hop in the shower. Are you two coming with?"

"No," said Martinique. "We'll stay here and come without you."

"Y'all are gonna fuck like bunnies while I take care of business? No fair." But Cyl was laughing. She was glad she had these two and was happy they had each other when she had to be elsewhere.

Cyl dropped the keys off with the Realtor, signed some papers, and headed back to the hotel. They still had some time before they had to get to the airport and she was hoping to partake in more pussy before they had to leave.

She found Martinique and Luna sound asleep when she got there. She thought about waking them since she was horny as hell, but decided to get things packed up and just let them sleep until it was time to get ready.

Cyl was packing the last suitcase when she heard moaning and she went into the sleeping area to find Luna fingering herself. Cyl climbed onto the bed, took one of Luna's voluptuous breasts in her mouth and plunged her fingers deep within her.

"Yes, stud. Fuck me like only you can."

Cyl continued to slip and slide inside and out until Luna called her name as she reached the pinnacle of pleasure.

"Okay, you two," Cyl said. "We need to get a move on. Get yourselves ready to fly."

Cyl stripped and took another shower with Luna and Martinique and she took each one to another orgasm before the water started to turn cold. It was time to fly home. Cyl was saying good-bye to Fort Collins for the last time. And she couldn't have been happier.

Chapter Twenty-seven

Cyl saw she had five missed calls when the plane landed in Tampa. She listened to her voicemail. Someone had broken into the lighthouse and also the cottage. She was fuming as she called the local precinct.

"This is Cyl Waterford. I got some calls that someone had broken into my place?

"One second, Ms. Waterford. I'll get you to the person handling the investigation."

Cyl was on hold for what seemed like an eternity before a gruff sounding officer barked into the phone.

"I've been trying to reach you. Do you not answer your phone?"

"I was on a plane back from Colorado." Cyl tried to remain calm. "Now can you tell me what happened?"

"Yep. We got three people who broke into your lighthouse. We caught them as they were trying to get into your house. Luckily, some kids were heading out that way for a make out session. They saw them and called it in."

"Shit. Did they get anything?"

"We don't think so," he said. "But we'll need you to come to the station to press charges."

"We're on our way."

"What happened?" said Martinique.

"Someone busted into the lighthouse. They were trying to get into the cottage when the cops pulled up. We need to go by the cop shop so I can press charges."

"Who would want to break in to our place?" said Luna.

"I have to assume it was Tawny," Cyl said. "She's top of my list of potential suspects."

"God, I hope not," Luna said. "I mean, would she really stoop that low?"

"She tried before," Cyl pointed out. "Only this time no one was home to interrupt."

"Damn her to hell," said Martinique. "Damn her straight to hell."

The three of them entered the police station and asked to speak to Officer Fosset. He looked over the throuple and said, "Which one of you is Waterford?"

"That would be me." Cyl stepped forward. "Who did this officer? And why?"

Fosset laughed.

"I think they're high on something. The woman kept insisting you had sunken treasure that belonged to her." He shook his head. "Some people can't handle their narcotics."

Cyl forced a chuckle.

"I guess not. Do we get to see the would-be thieves?"

"I don't see why not. First, I need to know if you're going to press charges. Or would you like to meet with them and decide then?"

"Oh, hell no," said Martinique. "She's definitely pressing charges."

"Yes. Yes, I am."

"Great. Let's get the paperwork done."

Cyl answered all the questions and signed all the paperwork.

"Now can we see them?"

"Sure. There was a woman and two men. Who would you like to see first?"

"I'm mostly interested in the woman," said Cyl.

"Not surprising," Fosset said under his breath.

He left them in the hall outside of Tawny's cell.

"Jesus fucking Christ, I'm sick of the sight of the three of you," Tawny said.

"We're not too keen on you either," said Cyl. "Especially after you fucking broke into my lighthouse."

"Whatever." Tawny shrugged.

"Look," Martinique stepped closer to the cell. "You need to leave us the fuck alone and give up whatever delusions you have."

"Delusions? Look. That treasure is mine. I thought of it first. I started searching for it first. It's mine."

"That's where you're wrong," said Luna. "It's not yours. Not in any way, shape, or form."

"Bullshit. I'm sitting here for burglary when y'all were the ones who stole from me!"

"We didn't." Cyl spoke calmly. "We are pressing charges on you though. And when you get out, you'd better hope you see me before I see you or you'll be in a world of hurt."

"Whatever. I'll never give up trying to get what's rightfully mine."

"It's not yours, you fucking psycho bitch," Martinique said.

Tawny sat down on her bed with a smug look on her face.

"What?" said Luna.

"If I can't have it, nobody can."

"And what's that supposed to mean?" Cyl was tired and just wanted to get home.

"I'm going to report that you have sunken treasure. They'll come and take it away from you. I'm sure a museum would love that collection."

"A, You don't even know what's in the chest. B, No one is going to believe you about sunken treasure. C, We've checked. No one has claim to our treasure. Not a museum. No one."

"We'll see about that," said Tawny.

"Do what you've got to do," said Cyl.

"I hope you rot in here," said Luna.

Cyl signaled to the guard that they were ready to leave.

Fosset met them.

"Did she mention the treasure?"

"Sure did," said Cyl.

"Any idea what she's talking about?"

"Not a clue," said Cyl.

"Drugs. I'm telling you," said Fosset.

"I guess," Cyl said.

They thanked him for his help and made their way out to the parking lot where they waited for their Uber.

"It'll be nice not to have to worry about Tawny anymore," said Luna.

"Ain't that the truth?" said Martinique.

"I don't know," Cyl said. "She makes me nervous with all her talk about the treasure."

"But no one believes her," Martinique said.

"What if they do, though? I mean, eventually?" said Cyl.

They rode back to the cottage in silence. It was late and Cyl should have been exhausted. Instead, she had a gnawing in her stomach, and she wasn't sure she'd be able to sleep until the treasure had been dealt with.

Once home, Martinique and Luna declared they were dead on their feet and headed for the bedroom.

"You two go on. I've got work to do."

"What kind of work?" said Martinique.

"I'm gonna split up the treasure so we can hide it. I'll feel safer."

"You're going to do that now?" said Luna. "It's the middle of the night. Surely it can wait until tomorrow?"

"I'm afraid it can't. I'm too worried to sleep anyway. What if someone finds out the truth? What if they come here looking for it? We've got to hide it."

"Do you want our help?" Luna stifled a yawn. Cyl chuckled.

"No thanks. I mean, I appreciate the offer, but y'all get your beauty sleep. I'll handle things."

She kissed them both good night and popped the top on a cold one. She sat at the dining room table and stared at the overflowing treasure chest. How the hell was she going to hide all that?

Cyl knew it had to be done but drank her beer and racked her brain to come up with a how to. She was halfway through her second beer when she had an idea. She went into the laundry room and grabbed some black industrial garbage bags. Back at the table, she started filling them with jewels. It took ten bags, but finally the treasure chest was empty.

Now came the hard part. Cyl dragged the bags and positioned five of them throughout the cottage. She put some in the closets and they looked just like the bags of laundry that needed to be done or maybe clothes bagged for donation. That left her with five bags, and she knew what she had to do. She was tired by then, though, so left them in the dining room and went to bed.

Cyl awoke the following morning to an empty bed. She checked her watch. It was almost ten. Damn. She never slept that late. She quickly pulled on shorts and a T-shirt and went in search of Martinique and Luna.

They weren't in the kitchen or dining room or even the living room. They weren't home? But where would they have gone? She texted Martinique who replied that they were on the point. Cyl beelined it to the point where she found Martinique and Luna cuddled together, both naked as jaybirds.

"You had to come all the way out here to have sex?" Cyl laughed.

"We didn't want to wake you," said Luna.

"Besides," Martinique said, "we didn't set out to have sex. It just kind of happened."

"Imagine that," said Cyl.

"Join us?" said Martinique.

"Thanks, but I'd rather you two get dressed right now. We need to go get breakfast. I've got work to do today."

"Work?" Luna said. "What kind?"

"I'll explain. Let's get going though."

At the diner, Cyl explained what she had planned for the day.

"I'm going to bury the treasure along the point. Then I'm going to resod so it won't be noticeable."

"That sounds like a lot of work," said Luna.

"It will be. But it's what has to be done. If someone comes by looking for treasure, we can't be sitting there with it. They could take it away from us."

"We don't need the money so desperately, do we?" said Martinique.

"It's not the value that concerns me. It's the fact that it was Brigid's and it's like having a piece of her with us."

"That makes sense," Luna said.

They stopped at the hardware store and bought three shovels. Luna and Martinique had promised to help, though Cyl didn't know how much they'd actually do. They bought three pairs of gardening gloves, too, and headed home.

It took a few hours, with Cyl digging three holes and the others managing one apiece, but they got the treasure buried. Cyl took off and bought some sod and laid it out over the treasure holes.

"We really should put some kind of markers out here so we know where we buried it," said Martinique.

"That's a good idea," said Luna.

Cyl contemplated for a few and decided they were probably right.

"What should we get though?" she said. "They would need to be heavy to withstand wind yet decorative so it doesn't look suspicious."

They went to a garden store and found huge statues of different types of fish. They bought a swordfish, a sailfish, a dolphin, and two seahorses. They paid extra to have them delivered. With that taken care of, they went home for baths and booze.

Chapter Twenty-eight

Things settled into a nice routine once they were back from Fort Collins. Cyl got the master bathroom finished and began working on odds and ends to spruce up the cottage and the lighthouse. Martinique and Luna were back to their daily grind. Everything was peaceful and settled. If it wasn't for the treasure chest under the table, Cyl might have been able to convince herself that Brigid and Aurnia were parts of a dream she'd had.

One evening after Luna and Martinique had come home from work, Luna told them she needed a favor.

"What kind of favor?" said Cyl.

"I want you to come to Oaklawn with me. Help me call Brigid and Aurnia. I want to do a show on them."

"No way," said Cyl. "You're not filming me calling Brigid."

"Why not?" said Martinique. "I don't mind. I think it would make a great piece. And what if we got to talk to Aurnia, too? How cool would that be?"

"I'd feel like an idiot," said Cyl. "Can't one of your assistants call them?"

"Brigid knows us," Luna said. "She's more likely to respond to us. You could keep your back to the camera. I really want to call them, but I think it needs to be the three of us."

"I agree," Martinique said. "She's more likely to make herself known if it's the three of us. Come on, Cyl. Like Luna said, keep your back to the camera. No one would know it's you."

Cyl knew it was futile to resist. She didn't want to do this as much as she'd love to "see" Brigid again. And the chance to meet Aurnia was a definite draw.

"When are we doing this?" she finally said.

"Oh, Cyl, you're the best." Luna hugged her tight.

"She has a good point," said Martinique. "When are you plan on doing this?"

"Next Friday night? If I can get permission from Oaklawn. But I don't think that will be a problem. We did a show there once years ago just to see if it was haunted. But now we know it is." She broke into a wide smile.

"That we do," Cyl said. "Next Friday night sounds good."

Friday night rolled around and Cyl grabbed the beer and wine to take out to the car.

"We'd better not take that," said Luna.

"Why not?"

"Oaklawn is sacred land or whatever. They don't like alcohol there."

"Fine. Then I'll bring a flask. And what about rum for Brigid?"

"I suppose that will be okay."

"Good."

They set up their table next to Aurnia's grave and began calling them. Cyl was uncomfortably aware of the camera crew and couldn't believe she'd agreed to this. After forty five minutes, Cyl was about to throw in the towel when there was a knock on their table.

"Brigid? Is that you?" said Luna. One knock.

"Are you alone?" said Cyl. Two knocks. "Is Aurnia with you?" One knock.

Cyl felt her heart skip a beat. She was so happy Aurnia and Brigid were together again after centuries apart.

"Hi, Aurnia. I'm Martinique. This handsome woman is Cyl and the beauty conducting this is Luna."

Cyl felt a strange mixture of cool and warmth wash over her. She wondered if Aurnia had hugged her. She was about to ask when the pen hovered over the paper.

Aurnia thanks you.

"It was our pleasure." Cyl had forgotten all about being on film. She forgot this was for Luna's show. All that mattered was that Aurnia and Brigid were back together, and she had helped make that happen.

"Can you hang out a while?" Luna said. One knock.

"I want you to know we sold some of your treasure," Martinique said.

Your treasure.

"That's right," said Cyl. "You gave it to us. And we'll put it to good use."

Enjoy it.

"We will," said Luna. "Though I do feel guilty that it's not with you."

Yours now.

"I don't know how we can ever thank you for that," Martinique said.

Aurnia's here. That's enough.

"I'm so glad you two are together again," Cyl said. "That makes me so happy."

There were two knocks on the table.

"You're not happy?" said Martinique.

Tired now.

"Okay," said Luna. "We'll let you go. Take care of each other please." One knock.

And then the air warmed up and Cyl knew they were gone.

"That's a wrap," said Luna.

"Oh, shit. I forgot you were filming."

"So did I for a bit. I was so happy that those two found each other again thanks to us," Luna said. To her crew, she said, "Did you get the writing? The knocking? Everything?"

"Everything," said a young woman. "I've got goose bumps."

"Don't we all?" said Martinique.

Cyl didn't move until the camera crew had dispersed. Yes, she was proud of all she had accomplished, but no she didn't want to be known as the architect who talked to ghosts. She got up and wrapped her arms around Martinique and Luna. She was so happy they'd found each other, and that together, they'd been able to reunite two star-crossed lovers.

"I'm so proud of us," Cyl said. "We did a really good thing."

"That we did," said Martinique. "Who knew we'd be able to help two ghosts find their forever partners?"

"Right? And, to think. Cyl didn't even believe in ghosts when we first met. I remember our first fight. She wouldn't let me do a piece on the haunted lighthouse."

Cyl laughed.

"I still wouldn't want you to, but at least now I get it. I really get it. Ghosts are real. I'm still in a small state of shock."

"You'll get used to it with Luna around," said Martinique. "She'll never let you forget it."

"Speaking of Luna being around," said Cyl. "I've been thinking."

"Should we be scared?" Luna said.

"Not at all. At least, I don't think so. I was thinking you two should sell your places and move into the cottage. I mean, y'all practically live there as it is."

"There's no room for all our stuff," Martinique said. "Apart from that though, I love the idea. And I'm really honored and proud that you want that."

"I do. We can make it work. I can add on. There's room for another living room and maybe a closet or two. At least think about it."

"I don't think there's room for another whole living room. Besides, we're talking two complete households converging on the cottage," said Martinique.

"There's room. Trust me. And what there's not room for we'll put in storage."

"That's an expense I don't need," Luna said.

"Two words. Treasure. Chest."

"You drive a hard bargain, Cyl Waterford," said Martinique.

"At least promise me you'll think about it. Both of you."

"Of course," said Luna. "I'm ready now."

"Seriously?" Martinique said. "So I'm the only holdout?"

"Apparently so," said Cyl.

"Shit."

"No hurry, Martinique. Just think about it. In the meantime, we'll get Luna moved after I make the changes to the cottage."

"I still can't believe you are offering," Martinique said. "Like, you really want this, don't you?"

"I do."

"Me, too," said Luna.

"I want it too," said Martinique. "I just can't see the logistics."

"We'll make it work. Let's go home and you two can tell me exactly what I need to build."

"Sounds good. Let's get home," said Luna.

They walked through the cottage measuring places for new closets and the space for the new living room.

"I have a walk-in closet in my condo," said Martinique. "So a little closet won't do me any good. See? I just don't know."

"What if we add on another bedroom, too? Or at least add a walk-in closet to the master? That would work, wouldn't it?"

"I'm exhausted," Luna finally said. "I can't think any more. Let's go to bed and pick this up tomorrow."

"Excellent idea," said Cyl. "Let's get some shut-eye."

Cyl woke before the other two and quietly slid out of bed to make the coffee. She was sipping her first cup when she heard Luna stretch. She knew it was Luna because Martinique never mewled as she stretched. She poured two cups of coffee and took them in to the room.

"Good morning, you two," she said.

"Sh," said Luna. "Martinique is still sleeping."

"Oh." Cyl lowered her voice. "Well, here's some coffee for you."

"I know what I'd rather have this morning."

"What's that?"

"You. Climb back into bed."

"We'll wake her," Cyl said.

"I'm sure she won't mind."

"Let's go into the spare room. I'd feel better."

They got comfortable on the spare bed and started making out like teenagers. Cyl couldn't believe how simply kissing Luna got her all hot and bothered. She was majorly turned on and had to take Luna soon.

She kissed down Luna's body, stopping to feast on her large breasts before kissing lower to where her legs met. Cyl stared for a long while, enjoying the glistening pink beauty before her, before she lowered her mouth to taste Luna's unique flavor.

"Mm," Cyl moaned, lost in the deliciousness of Luna as well as the juicy feel of her on her tongue. The sensations almost caused Cyl to short-circuit. She came close but managed to maintain her focus.

"Holy shit, you feel good," said Luna. "Oh fuck, Cyl."

Cyl grinned to herself with pride. She loved how easy it was to please Luna. But Luna deserved to get off so Cyl slipped her fingers in her while she licked and sucked her clit. Luna let out a blood curdling scream that Cyl was sure Brigid and Aurnia could hear, then collapsed on the bed.

"Damn that was awesome," Luna said. "Like wow!"

"Good."

"Give me a minute. I need to trust my legs."

"Why?"

"I just do."

Cyl waited impatiently until Luna got up.

"I'll be right back," she said.

"Are you going to wake up Martinique?"

"No."

Luna came back with Cyl's dildo. Cyl opened her eyes wide.

"Are you driving? Or am I?" she said.

"Oh, stud, you lay back and spread wide. I'm going to fuck you senseless."

At first, Luna licked and sucked Cyl's lower lips and everything in that region. Then she sat up and spread her legs.

"Can you see me?" she said. Cyl managed a nod though she was trembling uncontrollably. She was so fucking close and needed Luna to send her over the edge.

Luna surprised Cyl by burying the dildo deep inside herself. It disappeared from sight.

"Holy shit," said Cyl. "What are you doing?"

"Getting it ready for you."

"I think it's ready," said Cyl.

Luna grinned, slid the dildo out and sucked it clean.

"Fuck me. I'm going to please myself. You just keep doing that," said Cyl.

"No way."

Luna moved quickly for a larger woman. She rammed the dildo deep inside Cyl then slowly slid it out and plunged it in again.

"Is that what you wanted?" Luna said.

"Hell yes."

Cyl felt outstanding. She'd never been so full, and every time Luna dragged the silicone cock out, she dragged it over Cyl's throbbing clit. She knew she couldn't hold on much longer and quit trying to. She gave herself over to Luna. She was quaking as she teetered on the edge of oblivion. One final, powerful thrust and that was all she needed. She catapulted into orbit where she stayed for a few seconds before settling back into herself.

Luna sucked and licked the dildo clean then Cyl took it from her and teased her with it. She eased the tip inside, twisted it, and pulled it back out.

"Oh, no you don't," said Luna. "Give it to me or so help me God I'm going to go wake Martinique to finish me off."

Cyl laughed.

"Yes, ma'am."

She fucked Luna like she would never get to fuck another woman. And Luna rewarded her by crying out once, twice, three times.

"Now that is how you treat a woman," said Luna.

"Yes, ma'am," Cyl repeated before dozing off.

Chapter Twenty-nine

Cyl got all the permits and was hard at work adding on to the cottage. Luna had already pretty much moved in, and Martinique was in the process. Cyl's heart had never felt so full. She was extremely happy. In a way she'd never even dared to dream. Her days were full of improving the cottage, making it better for her two women and her nights were full of passion. What more could she ask for?

One night after dinner, she was snuggled on the couch with Luna and Martinique. She was feeling both content and restless. Content because she was right where she needed to be but restless because being so close to the two of them sent her hormones racing.

"Are you going to open an office here?" Martinique asked.

"That's the plan. I want to rent a space in Ybor City. But I want to get this place finished first."

"But do you really have to work?" Luna said.

"I'd go batshit crazy if I didn't work."

"But you haven't worked for all these months now."

"True. But I've stayed busy. What would I do if I didn't work?"

"Good point," said Martinique. "I know how you feel."

"I'm just curious. Because we have enough treasure to support us, really," Luna said.

"Then you can stay home," said Cyl. "If you want, I mean. Would you be willing to give up your show?"

"I might be. Or at least cut back on it. Maybe work three days a week."

"And what would you do the other two?" said Cyl.

"Lie around masturbating and fantasizing about you two." Luna laughed.

"That sounds like a great way to spend time off," Martinique said. "Maybe I'll go part-time, too."

"Let's all just quit our jobs and have sex twenty-four-seven," Cyl said.

"Now you're talking." Luna kissed Cyl. Hard. And Cyl's whole body responded. She eased Luna back on the couch and climbed on top of her. She ground into her, desperate for more.

"Don't forget me." Martinique pulled Cyl off Luna and kissed her.

"Oh, shit," said Cyl. "Everyone naked and in the bedroom. Now."

"Not so fast, stud," said Luna.

"What?"

"You get naked and get on the bed. Martinique and I will undress each other for you."

"Holy fuck. Now you're talking."

Cyl lay naked and watched as Luna and Martinique kissed each other and fumbled to remove each other's clothes. It was so fucking hot to watch. Breasts were bared and fondled, kissed and sucked. Cyl was a throbbing mess. When skirts and panties came off, Cyl thought she might self-combust. She'd never been so aroused. It seemed these two were intent on seeing how horned up they could get her. And they got her very horned up.

Luna was first to climb onto the bed with Cyl. She lowered herself onto Cyl's face while Martinique buried her tongue inside Cyl. Cyl devoured Luna's pussy. She was so hot and so wet and tasted like a woman should.

Cyl was beginning to lose her ability to think coherently as Martinique worked her magic on Cyl. Cyl struggled to hold on until Luna screamed and collapsed forward on Cyl. Cyl felt Martinique's fingers enter her and knew she wasn't far from her climax. Martinique lapped at Cyl's clit and that was all it took. Her world exploded into tiny little pieces as she came hard and fast.

Consciousness returned and Luna was between Martinique's legs. Cyl rolled over and sucked Martinique's nipple. She loved how it hardened in her mouth. She sucked harder and licked around it.

She slid her hand lower and rubbed Martinique's hard, slick clit. It was so covered in juices it made it hard to rub, but Cyl persisted until Martinique cried out and she reached her orgasm.

"See?" said Luna when they were all entwined, enjoying their postcoital bliss. "Every day could be spent doing that."

Cyl laughed.

"You drive a hard bargain, Luna."

"And think of the money we'd save," said Martinique. "No need for clothes. Ever."

"Mm. Good point," Cyl said. But she was getting drowsy. She tried to stay awake for the rest of the conversation, but sleep overtook her.

She awoke the next morning to an empty bed. Clearly the other two had decided to keep their day jobs. At least for the moment. Cyl smiled as she got up and started her day. She finished up the add-on that day and was ready to help the others move their furniture.

Two walk-in closets had already been built so the cottage was ready. It was done. She took a shower and headed down to Ybor City. She popped in to see Martinique who came out of her office.

"This is a nice surprise," she said. "To what do I owe this pleasure?"

"I was hoping for a little afternoon delight." She watched Martinique's eyes grow wide and laughed. "Actually, I was hoping you could give me the name of a Realtor or someone I could talk to about renting some office space around here."

"You're serious?"

"I am."

"Wow, Cyl. Come on to my office. I have some numbers in there."

Martinique's office had glass walls and that was the only thing that stopped Cyl from taking her right then and there. She looked so hot in her professional garb and Cyl wanted her with a desire that came from deep within.

Martinique jotted down three phone numbers.

"Any of these people would be able to help you. And stop looking at me that way or I'll take you into a restroom right now."

"Promises, promises."

"Come on."

Cyl followed Martinique down a hall. The way Martinique's hips swayed under her tight dress had Cyl growing wetter by the moment. They got to a spacious unisex bathroom and Martinique closed the door.

Cyl pulled Martinique to her in a passionate kiss and slipped her hand under her dress. She found Martinique ready for her, as usual. Cyl slipped her fingers deep inside then withdrew them and plunged in again. When Cyl's fingers were coated with Martinique's juices, she slid them out and pressed them into her swollen clit. Martinique buried her face in Cyl's shoulder as she moaned her release.

"What a pleasant afternoon this turned out to be," Martinique said.

"Indeed."

Cyl kissed her again then Martinique opened the door and led her back to the lobby.

"I'm sure one of them can help," she said. "If not, let me know."

It was four o'clock by then and Cyl debated waiting to call. Instead, she went to her favorite pub and called one of the numbers.

"Silveira Realty."

"Hi. My name is Cyl Waterford and I'm looking for an office to rent in Ybor City."

"You've come to the right place. Let me get you to a Realtor."

"Thank you."

Cyl sipped her Guinness while she was on hold. A voice that sounded like an older woman came on the line.

"This is Nadine McKinney. I understand you want to rent an office in Ybor City?"

"I do. I'm an architect and I need to set up shop here in Tampa. I'll need a nice office."

"I have some properties I can show you," said Nadine. "When would you like to meet?"

"What are you doing right now?"

"Right now? Oh, my. Well, it's short notice, but I suppose I can meet you."

She gave Cyl an address and said to be there in fifteen minutes.

Cyl didn't like the locations of the first two she saw.

"The next property is very pricey," said Nadine. "But it sounds like what you're looking for."

The office space was on the first floor on a main street. It was large and perfect.

"This is the one I want," said Cyl.

"You haven't even asked me how much rent is."

"It doesn't matter. I'll take it. Can we fill out the paperwork tonight?"

"Yes. My office is in walking distance. May I ask what brought you to Tampa?"

"My aunt passed away and left me her property, a lighthouse and cottage. I've been fixing them up, but now I'm ready to go back to work."

"The lighthouse? Are you Marjorie's niece?"

"I am indeed." Cyl was blown away, yet again, that everyone seemed to know her aunt.

"Well," Nadine beamed. "It's a pleasure and a privilege to be able to help you."

"Thank you."

Cyl filled out the paperwork. She hadn't worked in months, but the money from the sale of her condo was in her bank, so she had no doubt she'd be approved. She filled out what her usual monthly income was, listed Martinique and Luna as references, as well as a former client in Fort Collins, and she was through.

"When can I pick up the keys?" she said.

"Assuming everything checks out, you'll get the keys Monday."

"Thank you, Nadine," Cyl shook her hand. "Thank you very much."

"It's been a pleasure working with you. I'm excited to know Marjorie's niece will be using that office space."

As Cyl walked back to her car, her phone buzzed a couple of times. It was Luna.

Where are you?

Just rented an office. Be home soon.

"We need to celebrate," Cyl said when she walked into the house. "Let's go out for dinner and drinks, I'm buying."

"That sounds good. I take it you found a place?" said Martinique.

"Wait. How is it that you knew she was looking for a place today and I didn't?" said Luna.

"She came by my office to get names of Realtors."

"And I did find a place. A ground floor awesome space. I've already filled out the paperwork and paid first and last month's deposit. I should get the keys Monday. Come on, you two. Off the couch. Let's get some food and drinks in us."

They Ubered back to Ybor City so Cyl could show them where her office would be. Then they found a Cuban restaurant where Luna and Martinique had mojitos and Cyl had cuba libres. They ordered their food and ate and drank until it was nine and Martinique and Luna announced they had to get home since they had work the next morning.

"Bummer," said Cyl. "But, okay. We can get home."

They were going through their nighttime routines. Cyl stood in the bathroom doorway while Luna and Martinique removed their makeup and brushed their teeth.

"I love our life," said Cyl.

"Me, too."

"Me, three."

Cyl thought for a minute. She had something else she wanted to say but wasn't sure how well it would go over. She decided not to say anything.

Later, they were all snuggled together in bed and Cyl couldn't hold it in any longer.

"There's something I need to tell you two. It isn't easy for me, but I really want to say it. Please don't get upset or anything. Just let me say it and you can think on it, okay?"

"Are you leaving us?" said Luna.

"What is so important?" said Martinique. "You're scaring me."

Cyl let out a deep breath. She was scared, too, but had to do it. Before she could change her mind, she blurted out.

"I love you two. I have for a long while but I've been afraid to say it. I know y'all are just having fun or whatever, but I have fallen head over heels for both of you."

"Are you serious?" said Martinique.

"Look," Cyl said. "Don't react negatively without thinking it over."

"No," said Martinique. "There's nothing to think over. I love you two, as well."

"As do I." Luna had tears streaming down her face. "Oh, my God. I'm so happy to finally be able to say that out loud."

"Are you two sure?" said Cyl.

"Positive," they answered in unison.

"Then let's stay together forever."

"Yeah. Like Aurnia and Brigid forever," said Luna.

"Exactly like that," said Martinique.

"Yeah." Cyl's heart was full. Life hadn't turned out like she'd expected. In any way, shape, or form, but she wouldn't trade it for anything in the world. She'd found happiness.

Epilogue

Cyl woke early one morning to the sights and sounds of Luna and Martinique making love. She was very tempted to join in, but she had a deadline, so needed to get to the office. She tore herself away from the beauties she could watch all day and got in the shower. After the shower, she grabbed a coffee to go and drove to her office in Ybor City.

As she let herself in, she reflected yet again on the past two years. Had she really been in Tampa that long? She couldn't believe how much life had changed…how much *she'd* changed. Life was a crazy journey. That was for sure.

She started the coffee in her office and sat down to finalize the plans for Brenda Jensen's estate that would be located just outside of Tampa's metropolitan area. Brenda was terrified of hurricanes so Cyl had done her best to design a building that would be able to withstand a variety of wind shears. Of course, some hurricanes took out whole houses regardless, and Cyl had explained that to Brenda, but she'd been adamant about the design.

So Cyl had done what Brenda wanted. She checked the clock. It was almost two. Brenda would be there any minute. Cyl cleaned up her workspace and sat, ready for her client.

Brenda Jensen sauntered in a fifteen past. She was an older woman with eccentric taste who always made Cyl smile.

"Are the plans for my place ready?" Brenda said with no preamble.

"They are. May I get you a cup of coffee?"

"No. Let's just look at my plans."

Cyl led Brenda to the viewing room. It was set up like a living room with couches and wingback chairs with a large drawing table in the center where plans could be viewed.

"Oh, my, Cyl. This looks lovely. But I have no idea what I'm looking at."

Cyl grinned. She proceeded to explain the drawing to Brenda who oohed and ahhed. She was sold. She paid Cyl a hefty sum then left with the plans to go see her contractor.

Score! Cyl was thrilled it had gone so well. Her business as an architect was booming and Brenda Jensen had just given it even more of a boost. Cyl was restless though. She wanted to celebrate. She had more plans to work on but had no desire. She heard the bells on the front door and hurried out to see who her next client would be.

She stopped and smiled at the sight of Luna and Martinique, each wearing skimpy dresses and looking absolutely delectable.

"To what do I owe this pleasure?" Cyl kissed one then the other.

Martinique backed up and Cyl heard the front door lock slide into place.

"Is everything okay?" Cyl said.

Martinique smiled devilishly.

"How did your meeting go with your client?" Luna said.

"It went wonderfully. As a matter of fact, I was hoping to take you two out for dinner to celebrate."

"We had another celebration in mind," said Martinique.

"You did?"

"Mm. Let's go back to the viewing room."

Cyl felt the familiar butterflies in her stomach that arrived whenever she thought about making love to her women. She knew that's what they were getting at. Or, at least hoped it was.

She led them back to the makeshift living room.

"Is there no door to this room?" Luna said.

"Afraid not."

"Even better." Martinique grinned. "Lie on the couch, Cyl."

Cyl did as instructed. The rich leather under her felt good as it hugged her. Martinique unzipped Cyl's slacks while Luna unbuttoned her shirt. Soon Cyl was exposed on all fronts and was throbbing in anticipation.

Luna kissed Cyl hard on the mouth and Cyl arched off the couch to kiss her harder. She was lost in the kiss, in the feeling of Luna's soft tongue against hers, and it caught her completely by surprise when Martinique entered her. She moaned into Luna's mouth. Luna broke the kiss and nibbled down her neck to her chest. She sucked hard on one of Cyl's nipples and Cyl reflexively arched her hips at the feeling.

Martinique continued to fuck Cyl with her fingers until she finally took Cyl in her mouth. Martinique's tongue was so talented, and it didn't take any time until Cyl screamed, completely forgetting she was in an office building.

She opened her eyes to see both women staring at her with smug looks on their face.

"So was that the celebration? Is it over now?" said Cyl.

"Easy, stud. We're just warming up."

Martinique placed her knees on either side of Cyl's head, hiked up her dress, and lowered herself onto Cyl's face. Oh, shit yeah. Cyl loved eating Martinique. And when Martinique acted so wantonly, it only fueled Cyl's fire.

She had her tongue running laps all over Martinique's pussy. She was on her and in her. Luna kissed Martinique then and grabbed Cyl's hand. She placed it on her hot, wet center and Cyl plunged her fingers deep. It was hard to concentrate on both women at once, but what a wonderfully pleasant challenge. If Cyl had a heart attack right then, she would have died a happy woman.

She focused her attention on her women's clits and they both yelled her name as they found their release. Cyl was just getting warmed up. She wanted to take them again and again. She wanted them to fuck her senseless over and over. She wanted and needed to spend the afternoon making love to them.

Luna stepped back and helped Martinique off Cyl's face. Luna went to her purse and pulled out the dildo.

"Oh, yeah," said Cyl. "Oh, fuck yeah."

Martinique sat in one of the wingback chairs and spread her legs. Cyl had a perfect view of the heaven that lay between them. Luna sucked and licked the dildo like a pro. Then she eased it inside Martinique. Seeing Martinique take the whole thing made Cyl's clit swell to almost bursting.

Martinique cried out and Luna spun around and rammed the dildo, coated with Martinique's essence, inside Cyl. It happened so fast that it caught Cyl off guard. Still, it felt amazing. She arched her hips to take more and when Luna took Cyl's clit in her mouth, Cyl screamed again.

She came to and Martinique was using the dildo on Luna. Damn. The sight of that got Cyl all worked up again. It was a vicious cycle. One she wouldn't trade for anything.

By the time they had finished playing, it was four thirty.

"Let's get dinner," Cyl said. "We can keep the celebration going with steaks."

They straightened out their clothes and walked along Sixth Avenue until they arrived at the steakhouse. They placed their orders and sipped wine while they waited for their food.

"So, I've been thinking," said Cyl.

"Uh-oh," Luna said.

"I'm scared," said Martinique.

"Very funny. Now, seriously, hear me out. Look, I love you two. You know that, right?"

Luna and Martinique nodded.

"You're scaring me," said Martinique. "Is this where you tell us you're moving back to Fort Collins?"

Cyl grabbed her hand.

"No, babe. Nothing like that. The thing is…and I can't believe I'm saying this…but I think I'd really like to marry you two."

Martinique and Luna broke into wide smiles.

"Do you mean that?" Luna said.

"I do. But. And this is huge. Bigamy is not allowed here. It's against the law. However, maybe what we need to do is have a commitment ceremony. Y'all have your friends. And I've made a few friends since I've been here. What would you say to a commitment ceremony?"

The waitress arrived with their salads, so Cyl had to wait for their replies.

"I think that's a great idea," said Luna. "And I'm sure I could find someone to officiate."

"Awesome," said Cyl. "And you? Martinique?"

"I'm verklempt. I don't even know what to say."

"Say you want to be formally committed to us."

"Yes. Without a doubt."

"Sweet," said Cyl. She raised her wine glass. "To us."

"To us," Luna and Martinique said. They clinked glasses and took a sip.

As they ate their salads, Cyl listened, amused, as Martinique and Luna discussed rings and dresses.

"What about you?" Martinique said to Cyl. "You'll wear a ring, too, won't you?"

"I will. But it doesn't have to match yours. Y'all can get something feminine if you want."

"No," said Luna. "They'll have to match each other. We'll have to have a happy compromise."

"I know," said Martinique. "After dinner, let's go ring shopping."

Nothing sounded less entertaining to Cyl. But Luna nodded enthusiastically so Cyl knew she'd have to go along.

"All right. But we can't spend hours in jewelry stores," she said. "We're only looking for rings, okay?"

"Sure thing, stud," said Martinique. "We won't make you suffer too much."

"Appreciate that."

After dinner, they crossed over to the jewelers area of Ybor City. They searched through two stores and came up empty.

"Okay, ladies," Cyl said. "This has got to be the place."

She found one she liked immediately.

"Hey. Let's get Jose Gaspar rings."

"No." Martinique was firm. "But, what we could do is get rings made with the symbol of the *Tainted Rose* on them."

"That's a great idea," said Luna.

Cyl thought about it. Wearing a rose for the rest of her life? But it would honor Brigid and Aurnia by extension. So it would honor an ancestor. And she couldn't think of anything better.

"Great idea," she said.

They showed the jeweler the picture of the faded flag. She said she would be able to replicate it. They got their fingers measured, selected titanium, and headed on their way.

"How did y'all get here?" Cyl said. "Did one of you drive?"

"Nope. We Ubered. So we'll need a lift from you."

"That would be my pleasure."

They arrived home where they grabbed some drinks and cuddled together on the couch.

"I miss Brigid," said Luna.

"I do, too," said Cyl. "I often find myself wondering what she and Aurnia are up to. I ponder if they're finally happy together."

"We should go see her. Why not? What else are we doing right now?" said Martinique.

"We're relaxing," Cyl said. "The sun won't set for another hour to an hour and a half, and I, personally, plan to be in bed by then."

"Good point," said Luna. "Maybe Friday night?"

"Yeah," said Martinique. "Let's plan on that."

"You got it," Cyl said.

Luna got up and went to the kitchen. She came back with a bottle of wine.

"Who wants to go to the point?" she said.

"I'm up for that." Martinique stood.

"You coming, Cyl?" said Luna.

"You two just want to go out there and fuck like bunnies. We can do that here."

"If that were true, and I'm not saying it is, but if it were, wouldn't you at least like to watch?" Martinique said.

"Well, when you put it that way," said Cyl. "Let me grab a few beers."

They sat on the blanket and watched dusk settle over the city. Cyl had to admit, it was a beautiful city. It wasn't much bigger than Fort Collins, but it felt bigger. It felt more vibrant, more alive. Maybe that was just because she was with Martinique and Luna. She didn't know. Those two were so full of life. They made every day an adventure.

"I'm so proud of you, Cyl," said Martinique.

"Mm? How so?"

"You're making honest women out of us. I honestly didn't know you had it in you."

"Neither did I to tell the truth. But I love you two and I want the world to know we're a throuple. We'll be together until the end of time."

"I love the way you think," said Luna. "I can't imagine anyone else I'd rather spend my life with than you two."

"Amen to that," said Martinique.

They sat in silence for a while until Martinique and Luna started making out.

"Join us?" said Luna as she came up for air.

"What the hell?" said Cyl. "If I'm committed to you two crazy ladies, I'm committed in all forms."

"Good answer," said Martinique.

They made love until the sun went down then headed back to the cottage together.

Together, thought Cyl. Now and forever.

About the Author

MJ Williamz is the author of twenty-two published novels and several dozen short stories. Three of their novels have been Goldie winners.

The desire to write struck young and has never gone away. From California's Central Coast to Northern California to Portland, Oregon, to Houston, Texas, the need to put stories on paper has only grown and intensified.

MJ currently lives in Houston with their wife, fellow Bold Strokes Books author Laydin Michaels, along with three dogs and five cats.

Feedback? Feel free to reach out to mjwilliamz@aol.com.

Books Available from Bold Strokes Books

Broken Fences by Jo Hemmingwood. Former army sergeant Seneca Twist has difficulty adjusting to civilian life until she meets psychologist Robyn Mason and has a place to call home. (978-1-63679-414-3)

Never Kiss a Cowgirl by Ali Vali. Asher Evans dreams of winning the National Finals Rodeo in Vegas, and Reagan Wilson wants no part of something that brings back the memory of what killed her father. (978-1-63679-106-7)

Pantheon Girls by Jean Copeland. Cassie Burke never anticipated the detour life was about to take when a meeting with a prospective client reunites her with a past love and reignites the star-crossed passion they shared twenty years earlier. (978-1-63679-337-5)

Roux for Two by Aurora Rey. For TV chef Chelsea Boudreaux and hometown boy Bryce Cormier, love proves as tricky as making a good pot of gumbo. (978-1-63679-376-4)

Starting Over by Nance Sparks. Jennifer has no idea if she can mend Sam's broken soul after the sudden loss of her wife, but it's never too late for starting over. (978-1-63679-409-9)

The Accidental Bride by Jane Walsh. Spinsters Miss Grace Linfield and Miss Thea Martin travel to Gretna Green to prevent a wedding, only to discover a scandalous passion—for each other. (978-1-63679-345-0)

Three Wishes by Anne Shade. A magic lamp, a beautiful Jinni, and a cursed princess make for one unbelievable story. (978-1-63679-349-8)

Undiscovered Treasures by MJ Williamz. For Cyl and her friends Luna and Martinique, life's best treasures often appear when you're not looking. (978-1-63679-449-5)

Curse of the Gorgon by Tanai Walker. Cass will do anything to ensure Elle's safety, but is she willing to embrace the curse of the Gorgon? (978-1-63679-395-5)

Dance with Me by Georgia Beers. Scottie Templeton mixes it up on and off the dance floor with sexy salsa instructor Marisa Reyes. But can Scottie get past Marisa's connection to her ex? (978-1-63679-359-7)

Gin and Bear It by Joy Argento. Opposites really can attract, and as Kelly and Logan work together to create a loving home for rescue cat Bear, they just might find one for themselves as well. (978-1-63679-351-1)

Harvest Dreams by Jacqueline Fein-Zachary. Planting the vineyard of their dreams, Kate Bauer and Sydney Barrett must resist their attraction while battling nature and their families, who oppose both the venture and their relationship. (978-1-63679-380-1)

The No Kiss Contract by Nan Campbell. Workaholic Davy believes she can get the top spot at her firm if the senior partners think she's settling down and about to start a family, but she needs the delightful yet dubious Anna to help by pretending to be her fiancée. (978-1-63679-372-6)

Outside the Lines by Melissa Sky. If you had the chance to live forever, would you take it? Amara Rodriguez did, and it sets her on a journey to find her missing mother and unravel the mystery of her own heart. (978-1-63679-403-7)

The Value of Sylver and Gold by Michelle Larkin. When word gets out that former Boston homicide detective Reid Sylver can talk to the dead, the FBI solicits her help on a serial murder case, prompting Reid to assemble forces once again with Detective London Gold. (978-1-63679-093-0)

When It Feels Right by Tagan Shepard. Freshly out of the closet Marlene hasn't been lucky in love, but when it comes to her quirky new roommate Abby, everything just feels right. (978-1-63679-367-2)

Lucky in Lace by Melissa Brayden. Straitlaced stationery store owner Juliette Jennings's predictable life unravels when a sexy lingerie shop and its alluring owner move in next door. (978-1-63679-434-1)

Made for Her by Carsen Taite. Neal Walsh is a newly made member of the Mancuso crime family, but will her undeniable attraction to Anastasia Petrov, the wife of her boss's sworn enemy, be the ultimate test of her loyalty? (978-1-63679-265-1)

Off the Menu by Alaina Erdell. Reality TV sensation Restaurant Redo and its gorgeous host Erin Rasmussen will arrive to film in chef Taylor Mobley's kitchen. As the cameras roll, will they make the jump from enemies to lovers? (978-1-63679-295-8)

Pack of Her Own by Elena Abbott. When things heat up in a small town, steamy secrets are revealed between Alpha werewolf Wren Carne and her human mate, Natalie Donovan. (978-1-63679-370-2)

Return to McCall by Patricia Evans. Lily isn't looking for romance—not until she meets Alex, the gorgeous Cuban dance instructor at La Haven, a newly opened lesbian retreat. (978-1-63679-386-3)

So It Went Like This by C. Spencer. A candid and deeply personal exploration of fate, chosen family, and the vulnerability intrinsic in life's uncertainties. (978-1-63555-971-2)

Stolen Kiss by Spencer Greene. Anna and Louise share a stolen kiss, only to discover that Louise is dating Anna's brother. Surely, one kiss can't change everything…Can it? (978-1-63679-364-1)

The Fall Line by Kelly Wacker. When Jordan Burroughs arrives in the Deep South to paint a local endangered aquatic flower, she doesn't expect to become friends with a mischievous gin-drinking ghost who complicates her budding romance and leads her to an awful discovery and danger. (978-1-63679-205-7)

To Meet Again by Kadyan. When the stark reality of WW II separates cabaret singer Evelyn and Australian doctor Joan in Singapore, they must overcome all odds to find one another again. (978-1-63679-398-6)

Before She Was Mine by Emma L McGeown. When Dani and Lucy are thrust together to sort out their children's playground squabble, sparks fly leaving both of them willing to risk it all for each other. (978-1-63679-315-3)

Chasing Cypress by Ana Hartnett Reichardt. Maggie Hyde wants to find a partner to settle down with and help her run the family farm, but instead she ends up chasing Cypress. Olivia Cypress. (978-1-63679-323-8)

Dark Truths by Sandra Barret. When Jade's ex-girlfriend and vampire maker barges back into her life, can Jade satisfy her ex's demands, keep Beth safe, and keep everyone's secrets…secret? (978-1-63679-369-6)

Desires Unleashed by Renee Roman. Kell Murphy and Taylor Simpson didn't go looking for love, but as they explore their desires unleashed, their hearts lead them on an unexpected journey. (978-1-63679-327-6)

Maybe, Probably by Amanda Radley. Set against the backdrop of a viral pandemic, Gina and Eleanor are about to discover that loving another person is complicated when you're desperately searching for yourself. (978-1-63679-284-2)

The One by C.A. Popovich. Jody Acosta doesn't know what makes her more furious, that the wealthy Bergeron family refuses to be held accountable for her father's wrongful death, or that she can't ignore her knee-weakening attraction to Nicole Bergeron. (978-1-63679-318-4)

The Speed of Slow Changes by Sander Santiago. As Al and Lucas navigate the ups and downs of their polyamorous relationship, only one thing is certain: romance has never been so crowded. (978-1-63679-329-0)

Tides of Love by Kimberly Cooper Griffin. Falling in love is the last thing on either of their minds, but when Mikayla and Gem meet, sparks of possibility begin to shine, revealing a future neither expected. (978-1-63679-319-1)